The Pig War

MARK HOLTZEN

For Carolyn

ISBN: 1475051360
ISBN-13: 9781475051360

Library of Congress Control Number: 2012905011
CreateSpace, North Charleston, SC

1

This was Kell's first island. The word meant isolated, detached, and surrounded. *That sounds about right*, he thought. He stared off the edge of the dock and watched the ferry pull away into the blue-gray waters off of Orcas Island. The dock grew eerily quiet.

They had only seen photos of their Grandad. Kell had noticed only one thing—big bushy eyebrows. He scoured the dock and parking lot for them now.

Grace, his sister, was on top of a nearby concrete retaining wall, her red satin cape fluttering behind her in the wind. She pointed to the retreating ferryboat, "It has two fronts. How do you know which way it's going?" she asked, her arms spread wide.

"By looking at it," Kell snapped.

She jumped down, ran to him, and grabbed him in a big bear hug until he felt himself smile.

"Knock it off, goof," he said. Satisfied, she released him and ran to a piece of rickety fence to watch the ferry ease out of sight.

Kell walked to her and put a hand on her shoulder. "Gracie, the ferry has two ends so cars can drive in one end and out the other," he said.

"So the beginning turns into the end?" Grace asked.

"Its bow turns into its stern, yes," Kell said. Kell rubbed his head and took a deep breath; both often helped him calm down.

He saw a green sign with "Mobray Island" painted in white letters posted near a narrow ramp where a much smaller ferry was tied up. Kell knew they were to take a small passenger ferry to Mobray Island. No cars allowed. Their grandad was supposed to meet them here at the landing, but he was nowhere in sight.

This ferry was in desperate need of paint and rocked a little too much with each lapping wave. It had a tall structure in the middle, like a miniature air-traffic-control tower—for the captain, Kell guessed, to see where he or she was going. Two cars might have fit on the deck, had they been allowed, but the access ramp was only large enough for walk-on passengers. Kell looked with renewed eagerness for their Grandad, but saw no one waiting to board.

Kell took his hand from Grace's shoulder and turned toward the channel to look out onto the water. Further out, whitecaps rolled and tossed into one another. The sun shone through broken clouds, which cast their shadows onto gray waters. They looked dark, like patches of algae. The air was muggy and warm. His Grandad lived out there on an island somewhere. *Where is he?* Kell wondered.

●

Mobray Island was a mystery. It was where their mother had come from and his grandparents had remained. She rarely spoke of it. "I spent my childhood there," she'd say, "I'm a city girl now." Grandad supposedly didn't ever leave the island. So in order for their grandmother to see her grandchildren, she had visited Portland twice a year. She had died two years ago.

Grace set her bags down and put her hands on the ground while stretching her legs out straight with her bottom high in the air. She called it the giant triangle and learned it from their mom's yoga videos. She claimed it built her superhero flexibility. After scanning the area for a while, Kell set his bag down and sat on it. He told Grace she could fly within the boundaries of the ice cream stand and the edge of the ferry ramp. She agreed but ignored his boundaries anyway, creating a small whirlwind nearby.

Their mother had said Grandad would meet them. Kell wasn't sure what to do; he didn't want to board alone. They were children in a strange place; they couldn't just *go*. He stood up and paced toward, then along the edge of the dock, though not too close, for fear of falling in. He was supposed to take care of his sister, not go strange places without a chaperone. What if the ferry left before Grandad appeared? Would they have to spend the night on the docks?

Kell's stomach rumbled. It was almost lunchtime. He began to wonder what they would do for food. There was a drinking fountain nearby, so they would survive the night, but staying warm might be a problem. What if he didn't come tomorrow? They had each brought a jacket in case of rain showers but what about a thunderstorm? He knew Pacific Northwest weather was unpredictable. He continued to walk, waiting for something—anything—to change.

Grace explored the nearby rock wall. She wondered aloud if she could scale it without safety ropes. It would be her first summit of the day. Maybe she could do it twice before they had to leave.

After twenty minutes, Kell began to feel a mix of scared and furious. This was a disaster. Parents off in a foreign country, and an unknown grandfather who wasn't even there to pick them up.

After looking around a closed ice-cream shed he returned to find an orange-vested man leaning on the dock railing.

"You looking to go to Mobray?" he asked.

"Yeah," Kell mumbled. It annoyed Kell that this man wasn't busy.

"The last run of the day's leaving any minute," the man said, unaffected by Kell's tone. "No more until tomorrow morning."

Kell looked around again.

"You gonna sleep on the dock for the night then?" the man pushed.

Kell shrugged, "Don't want to, no."

Kell looked to Grace. She nodded, "Let's go, brother." Kell didn't know what else to do. He picked up his bag.

"Name's Evan, hop on board. We'll leave whenever the captain's ready," the man said.

They boarded the ferry.

"Who's the captain?" Grace asked while running her hand along the rope tying the boat to the dock.

Evan untied the rope, hopped onto the deck, and ran up to the captain's tower.

"Me," he said. The little boat's engine revved and they pulled out into open water. Kell watched as they left yet another dock behind. It was like they were hopping from rock to rock across a very large stream. *Grandad better be at the end of this ferry ride.* If he wasn't Kell wasn't sure what they were going to do.

•

Evan waved goodbye as they walked onto a rickety dock in need of repair. Coming across the channel, Kell had wondered how the small ferryboat would handle the choppy water. His stomach was a little queasy, but they hadn't tipped over. The dock looked like a sturdy but overused xylophone. Grace ran ahead and let out a whoop as she passed a small hand-lettered sign that read "Welcome to Mobray Island."

He looked past the sign to see Grace stopped where the dock met with a gravel road. She was staring at an ancient blue car. The dark green of the fir trees beyond it highlighted its washed out blue color. A gray-haired man sat inside with the door open.

Kell walked toward it. The car was pointed away from the forest, the front windshield facing out to the water. Through the window Kell could see two hands rested on the steering wheel and the silhouette of a head bobbing up and down, maybe in greeting, Kell wasn't sure. The man was leaned back in the seat and appeared to be chewing. He turned from time to time to follow motion on the water—a passing boat, a seaplane—reminding Kell of an otter floating on its back munching on an oyster or grooming itself. This otter, however, had thick, bushy eyebrows.

Kell tripped and landed hard on his left foot. As he caught his balance, Grace ran the short distance to the car. "Are you our grandad?" she said through the open window.

The head turned a little and continued to chew, "Yup."

Kell joined his sister and waited for Grandad to open the door, reach out his hand, offer to help with the bags, or at least make eye contact, but he saw only a slight shift of eyebrows. Wisps of gray hair and crooked wire glasses framed his face. He continued chewing.

"Why didn't you meet us at the ferry landing?" Kell asked.

"I did," he said.

A few moments passed, wakes from passing boats caused the ferry to bob up and down against the pilings. Not sure what else to do Kell looked toward the sound. He noticed Evan was in no hurry to make the return trip to Orcas. Grandad glanced at them now and again, but continued to look out onto the water. Even Grace seemed confounded by the scene. It didn't stop her from bouncing up and down in anticipation that something exciting could happen at any moment.

"Pshew," a sound came out of him like air from a tire. "Comin'?" he asked finally.

Kell picked up his bag and headed toward the car while the old man sat in the front seat.

Grace got into the back seat throwing her bag on the floor. "Your car is old," she said, looking over the interior.

"Yup," Grandad replied.

The car had likely been a deep and beautiful blue, but all that remained were blueish streaks along the top and sides. Silver chrome bands ran along the front edge of the hood, the edges of all four doors, and on top of two small fins that seemed to go on forever along the sides of the trunk.

Kell went to the other side, got in, and pulled his back door closed placing his bag next to him. Grandad had appeared more comfortable by himself looking out at the water. Now that he had company he shifted in his seat, not looking at or talking to them.

Their mom had told Kell that Grandad had some life-insurance money from their grandma's death. He used to be a house painter and handyman, but now he mostly gardened and fished. It sounded like laziness to Kell.

The front and back seats were long and slippery. Upon entering the car, Kell had instinctively reached across his body to buckle his seatbelt. There wasn't one. The first thing out of his mother's mouth when they got into any car was, "Seatbelts." He was annoyed at the lack of safety equipment, and also that he missed her voice so much.

Grace noticed, too. "There aren't any seatbelts."

"Mm-hm," Grandad shifted in his seat again.

As the car lurched, Kell thought of his parents. How could they abandon him to this? Why weren't they here to ease them into life with this stranger? They should have been introduced before, at least. The old man shifted down gears and the enormous, blue beast leaned around the corner onto a long gravel road.

If his mom were there, they would have discussed everything they would do on the vacation. Kell stared through the silence into the dark forest surrounding them. Strands of Grace's hair blew out the window. She beamed. He sulked.

As they made their way across the landscape it became evident that this wasn't his Pacific Northwest. His Portland house was surrounded by pruned flowering trees, ferns, and fresh bark chips. Their landscape-designer neighbor took care of the yard work.

Here on Mobray there were numerous ferns and fir trees like at home, but it was different. While boulders and trees covered the shore all the way to the waterline, the island's interior opened into wide fields of tall grass spotted with old houses. There were no well-pruned shrubs or tidy bark chips here. He couldn't tell if people were growing things or letting weeds take over. Old boats lay in one yard, two with paint flaking off. Huge rock formations and thick bunches of trees interrupted large meadows, in which clumps of taller green grass stood above the rest like missed hairs on a shaved head.

Gravel popped under the tires as they slowed to a stop. Kell wasn't sure why they were pulling over. All he saw was a rickety cabin and a bundle of trees. The old man creaked an odd handle on the steering wheel upward to park. Kell watched for any sign of communication. After a few seconds he realized no explanation or tour was coming, no helpful tips on how to get around or sights to see, even where to put their bags. They sat in the car. Everything seemed to move in slow motion.

"How did you get the car onto the island?" Grace asked. Kell had forgotten Grace was still in the back seat. He couldn't take his eyes from the scene, hoping this was just a quick stop on the way to their real accommodations.

Grandad looked at her in the rearview mirror and raised one eyebrow. "Yowzer," he said.

Grace smirked and giggled, somehow satisfied with his answer.

Kell noticed the small, triangle-shaped window near the front of the car that rotated out to let in the fresh air. The damp smell of earth wafted through. Kell looked again at the nearby cabin. *Oh, no, that's the house.*

Grandad's cabin was a brown-gray weather-beaten structure with wood shingles covering the sides, many hanging at an angle. It was a small rectangular box with two chimneys coming from the roof, one to the left side and one at the back. The roof didn't look as if it would leak, but was warped just the same. There were two windows at the front with a door in between. One window was larger than the other, forming a grotesque face with mismatched eyes, as if someone creepy was peering through a magnifying glass. The roof over the front porch sagged under a mat of thick green moss, which must have been gathering for years. The drooping rooflines seemed to echo his grandad's features. More patches of moss smattered the rest of the roof.

But it was the small building at the back of the property that especially troubled Kell. It was the size of a telephone booth with a crescent moon carved in the door. He had read about outhouses but never seen one, let alone used one. He hoped it was there purely for the purpose of showing "how it used to be."

"Wow," Gracie whispered. Her brown eyes opened wide.

Another building, narrower, sat a good distance behind the cabin and off to the right. Next to the shed was an open, chicken wire enclosure. A clump of trees towered to the right of it all, their branches swaying in a stiff breeze. Kell looked across at Grandad, then back at the house. It all matched somehow.

"Creepy," the word slipped from Kell's mouth. He clapped over it with his hand.

The little sound escaped his Grandad's lips again.

"Pshew."

Kell didn't know what the sound meant, but it didn't seem overly supportive.

"It's mine. Yours for a while. Get used to it," Grandad said.

2

The creak of the car doors echoed through the trees. Back home their mom often scolded Kell for slamming the car door too hard, but this one pushed back like Grace refusing to be pried out of his room. He gave it another try with his full body weight and the door finally slammed shut. The need to let out a big yawning stretch came over him, but he stifled the feeling.

The first things Kell noticed as he left the car were the sounds. Chirps, buzzes, and caws came from near and far. A hummingbird maneuvered above a shrub with small pink flowers and, as if it didn't like the company, zipped away.

They approached the front porch and an old black dog with gray hair around its eyes and snout raised its head. Two rocking chairs sat motionless on either side of it. The dog labored to its feet and padded toward Grace. It pressed its nose to her shin. She put her hand down and patted its head.

"He's smelly," she smiled at Grandad.

"Name's Crockpot," Grandad said, finally offering some information, one hand under a red suspender. The dog nudged Grace's hand and some snot spread across her palm.

Grace wiped her hand on her pants and turned away to look across the clearing. Crockpot walked to Grandad, nuzzled his hand and let him scratch his nose once, then sank back to the porch with a sigh.

Kell went back into the car, gathered the bags and lugged them to the porch. When he set them both near the front door he turned to ask Grace a question. She was gone.

"Where's Grace?" he asked. Grandad pointed out into the forest.

"Well, we need to find her," Kell pleaded.

"She'll be alright," Grandad said. "There aren't many places to go." And he turned to go into the house.

•

They had only been on the island a few minutes and he had already lost her. *Mom even warned me not to let her out of my sight.* He could make out the water through the trees. It was the only landmark he recognized so he headed in that direction. A tree branch rubbed against a neighboring trunk, moaning in the breeze. Vines reached for him and spindly branches tried to block his path. Spider webs tickled his face. After a few moments of silent listening he yelled his sister's name, but the only response was bird song and soft, far-off waves against a shoreline.

"Grace!" he yelled louder this time.

How had this happened? A few days ago they were at home in Portland, staying with family friends. Their parents were to be home from their research by late June in time for summer fun. Then a government went bad, rebels took over, and now Kell and Grace were marooned on Mobray Island. Kell had a bad feeling that his mom's "be home soon" was going to be longer than he wanted it to be.

Kell heard a twig snap behind him followed by what he thought was a muffled whisper. He whirled around. He stared for a long minute, but the only thing that stared back at him was a huge, toppled stump.

"Grace?" he said.

Silence. He was a little jumpy. The island, as peaceful as it seemed, was not home. A deep breath later he began to relax. The stump's huge roots formed a mangled wall next to him, leaving a huge hole where they had clung to the earth. He imagined the gusts of wind it would have taken to uproot it. Moss dangled from its trunk. A miniature chipmunk chirped a warning a few yards away. He returned his attention to his missing sister.

He had made a promise to his mom. What made matters worse was that Grace was off in the woods wearing her red satin cape. Superheroes had adventures and when they did, they weren't to be interrupted by anyone. Especially big brothers.

He had learned there was only one way to get her to answer in a situation like this.

"Hey, Annoyalator!"

When she wore the cape she demanded to be called her "rightful" name—The Annihilator. Making fun of it was often the only way to drag her out of hiding. He never enjoyed calling it out, especially with people around, but that didn't seem to be a problem here. He hadn't seen more than five people since they'd arrived and that included Grace and himself.

"Okay, only because I'm worried about you and I promised mom, you ridiculous nincompoop, ANNIHILATOR!"

Still nothing. He stumbled over a mossy, rotten log toward a small clearing.

"You are in so much trouble," he said to as if she were there. "Why don't you ever listen? Wander off the second we get here..."

A splintering sound engulfed him. His stomach shot into his throat. Air rushed past and he felt a sharp pain in his left elbow. He landed with a thud. His legs bent into his chest and hit his chin. He bit his tongue – hard. After a moment, he looked up through the darkness. Dust swirled everywhere. He was in a deep hole, about three feet wide. Towering above him on all sides was eight feet of dirt.

3

"Kell!" Grace's voice floated from above. The hole distorted the sound so he couldn't tell if she was nearby or far away.

"Kell!" she said again, this time sounding closer.

Finally she peered down from above. Sunlight backlit her tousled brown hair and sillouetted her face. Spots of red fabric were just visible behind her.

"Kell? What are you doing down there?" Grace yelled.

The cloud of dust made it hard to see and the taste in his mouth was a mixture of blood and dirt. His tongue was bleeding and he tried to keep it away from the sides of his mouth.

"I hate that shththoopid cape! Ow!" he screamed.

"Are you okay?" she asked. "You fell far."

"I think tho," he said, not entirely convinced. Things were hazy. He moved his arms, legs, and ankles.

"I'm gonna go find Grandad!" Grace's voice faded as she padded away.

"Wait! Grathie!" he yelled. He didn't want to be alone, but he definitely didn't want Grandad.

His first moments on the island and he was already hurt. He didn't like the thought of asking someone he didn't know for help, even a relative. Especially an old grumpy one. He wished their mom were here.

"Wait, jutht wait," he panted, hoping Grace could still hear him. "You don't even know where he ith, or where town ith, chust wait."

He sounded more confident than he was. Some courage seeped back when Grace reappeared in the circle of sky above.

He looked up the high wall of roots, rocks, and compacted dirt.

"You can get him thoon. Let me thee if I can get out firtht."

4

"I'm sorry, Kell, I know you get mad when I run off. I just wanted to start an adventure. Look, old boards. There are old boards broken where you fell in. Kind of grown over with grass though."

Kell could hear the muffled thuds of her jumping around. He took a deep breath and tried to clear his head.

"Kell? Kee-eell," she sang, her voice far away.

He felt the blood rush to his face.

"Because *you* wan off wiff that cape, *I'm* in thith hole! Now thut up!"

Kell felt guilty the minute he said it. But she had finally listened.

A nearby rock in the wall was big enough to grab so he yanked at it. It wiggled a little and gave him an idea. He pulled and twisted until it came loose, and then he shoved his foot inside the divot. He braced his right arm against the wall as he levered himself up with a grunt. The hole was cramped so he hit the wall behind him. His left arm hurt, but he used it also to hold himself at that height.

"What're you doing?" she asked. "Can I help?" As bothersome as she was, at least she seemed to be taking the situation more seriously. With another grunt he moved one foot, then the other, then he moved his hands up to a hole between some rocks.

"It smells funny down there," she said.

Kell ignored her.

"Kell?" Grace whispered.

"Working," he mumbled to Grace. He was beginning to adjust his speech to his swollen tongue.

He pushed his back against the wall behind him and put one foot up at a time in front of him. Little by little he scooted his shoulders up, then his feet, then his shoulders.

When he had risen four feet up the wall, his hand brushed against something that felt... he wasn't sure, but somehow unnatural. He put his legs in a position that felt secure and reached for it. He ran his hand along a smooth curved edge.

"That's weird," he said. "I think I found something."

•

"What?" Grace asked. She leaned over and knocked dirt down onto his head. "Sorry."

The thing felt like old wood, firm but slightly yielding. He pulled hard on the edge of the mysterious object and almost lost his balance. He yanked again, popping his feet off the wall. He fell to the bottom of the hole with a startled gasp. It wasn't far but he made sure to keep his injured tongue at the back of his mouth this time. He reached back up the wall and felt the thing, whatever it was. It was just below eye level and he could now barely see the outline. The hard, curved edge moved as he yanked it to the left then pushed back to the right. Side to side, back and forth.

He grabbed hard and yanked with his body. The object, about as big as his chest, popped from the dirt and tumbled against his knees to the ground below. Something thudded inside it. It was a barrel. He was tempted to open it, but wanted to get out of the hole first. Kell tried to lift it, to throw it out of the hole before resuming his climb, but it was surprisingly heavy. *The last thing I need is for it to fall down and bash me on the head,* he thought. But standing on end, the barrel was about two feet high. And it had left a nice big foothold for him in the dirt wall. Kell stood carefully on top of the barrel. He braced his hands against the side of the hole, found more large rocks as handholds, and lifted one foot into the barrel-shaped space. With the extra height, and a good strong lunge, Kell found himself able to reach the top of the hole. Grace squealed and grabbed at him as he scrambled up and out.

"I'm glad you're safe, Kell. You're a good big brother," Grace said.

"Yeah, well, the Annihilator just got me into a lot of trouble," he said with a stern look.

"I was scared for you," she said.

"It scared me, too, Gracie. Now throw away your cape," he said.

A grin spread across her face, "No." She pushed past him and looked back down the hole.

"What did you find? How come you didn't bring it up?"

"It was too big. Doesn't matter. We're safe now. Let's find Grandad before we get into any more trouble."

"What if it's treasure?" she squinted even harder, trying to make out the shape below.

He grabbed her arm, "Grace, I just got out of there. I don't need you falling in now. Let's go!" His eyes moved nervously to the spot where he had fallen. He noticed the old, rotten boards surrounding them, overgrown with tall brown grass. The way they lay suggested they may once have formed some kind of structure. He saw what looked like nail holes in the end of one. Boards were splintered where he had broken through. It looked less scary from up here, but there was no way he was going down in there again.

"We can't just leave it down there," she implored.

"We can," he replied. "And we will. Let's go." He began to walk away.

Of course, a part of him did wonder what a wooden barrel was doing at the bottom of a deep hole. And what was rumbling around inside it?

He stopped and turned to see his sister dragging a long branch toward the opening.

"Grace, no," he ran toward her and took hold of the branch.

"I'll get it, you open it, and we can see what it is," she said. She said it as matter-of-factly as if she were going to make a sandwich. "I'll come back later if you don't let me," she sang.

He knew it was true. She never gave up on things once she made up her mind. Once, when she was three, she had left the house and ridden her tricycle through two stoplights to get downtown because she *knew* she deserved a chocolate ice cream cone with sprinkle candy on top. When their parents, along with the sheriff, were glaring at her later, she had simply insisted she had to have it that day and couldn't wait a minute more.

"What's the use?" Kell sighed. "Okay, but it's too heavy for me to lift so there is no way you're going to be able to do it. Why don't you run to Grandad's to see if there is something lying around, a rope or something."

In a flash she was gone. A few minutes later she returned with a rope with a hook on the end.

"I snuck around the back of the house and found it by the chickens," she said. "Those chickens are so cute."

"Yes, I'm sure they are," he answered.

He helped her lower the branch she had found. It was just long enough to reach the bottom, leaving the high end two feet from the top of the hole.

She lowered a leg down and perched on the sturdiest upper limb. Then, balancing on one foot, she made an elegant arch with her arm and looked to the sky.

Kell rolled his eyes. Grace put on a goofy, open-mouthed smile big enough to to catch a small bird. His mom could have stopped her. She would have used *the tone* accompanied with *the look*.

Kell couldn't do either, so he used his hands and a foot to steady the branch as his sister hung off the next limb like a monkey and lowered herself into the pit. He lowered the rope after her.

5

As annoyed as Kell often was with his sister, he was amazed at her physical feats. She had scooted down the limb, secured the container with the rope, and climbed the limb to guide it while Kell pulled it up. She had even helped push it with her head during a couple of tricky spots. The old barrel now lay in front of them, and they stared at if something alive were going to emerge from it. The edges that Kell had felt were two circular ends. Grace was on her knees running her hands over it as if it were a brand new toy.

Kell had never given a barrel much thought. It was a basic thing that just *was*. He saw them in antique stores and barns holding old rakes and broken shovels. On closer inspection it was actually pretty cool. It was made of pieces of curved wood tightly fitted together and secured by metal bands at the top and bottom. He couldn't find any cracks. There were scratches and scrapes along the sides, but for the most part it was solid. This one seemed sealed tight enough to hold liquid. Something heavy slid and thudded inside when he rolled it back and forth.

Grace let out a blood-curdling shriek. Kell looked up to find her twenty feet away with a crazy look in her eyes. He backed away and watched her run from across the meadow until she became a brown-haired blur. She leapt into the air and bounced off the top of the barrel, skidding to a stop back at Kell's feet. The pile of tangled hair, twigs, and red cape looked up and grinned. As the barrel rocked back and forth, he could still hear the sound coming from inside. He picked up a thick branch. It was Grace's turn to back away as he took a huge swing.

He brought the limb down, hard. The instant it struck it bounced back high into the air, pointing to the clouds. His hands went with it and sang like tuning forks. He dropped the stick and shook his arms, whining like a four-year-old.

After regaining his composure, he attempted four more swats, cheered on by a caped crusader. The strength of the barrel impressed him. It rolled with each new strike, until finally a partially rotten board gave. A few more blows reduced it to a pile of loose boards and metal loops.

He and Grace stood in the middle of the broken pieces and the two hand-pounded metal bands. At their feet lay a piece of oilcloth wrapped around a lump of something heavy. Grace squatted down and began to unroll it. An ancient-looking, rusted pistol tumbled from the cloth.

"A gun!" Grace said.

"Yeah," Kell whispered, his eyes wide.

Kell bent down and ran his finger along the handle. He had never touched a real gun.

"What do we do?" she asked, looking at him.

He had no idea. The questions began to line up in his mind. Who put it in a barrel? Had it killed anyone? What *were* they going to do with it?

"It's so cool," Grace cooed. "Treasure. We found treasure, Kell!"

"We have to hide it," Kell said.

His sister stared at him in disbelief.

"We have to hide it and not tell anyone."

19

6

"Really? Isn't that bad?" she asked. Her initial look of surprise morphed into a sly grin.

Kell knew she had reason to be surprised. He did his homework as soon as he got home from school. He ate the healthy snacks his mom put out for them. He turned in his assignments on time. If kids were fighting on the playground he was the first to find a teacher.

He wasn't sure why he didn't want to tell his grandad. A big reason was that he was scared. Kell had never been around a gun. His parents watched the news; he saw articles in the newspaper. Guns were dangerous.

Plus he was mad. He'd had plans for the summer. Hang out with his friends, read whatever he wanted, and do some research at the library. Now his parents were stuck in a strange country and his plans were stuck there with them. He knew it wasn't anyone's fault. He had no reason to take it out on anyone, but that didn't make him feel any less miserable and angry. If he always did what he was supposed to do and things still didn't turn out how he wanted, then what was the point in being good?

On top of that, he didn't trust his Grandad. They barely knew the man. Kell would have taken it to his parents immediately, but not to the cranky old guy who lived in a shack and seemed to have no interest in actually taking care of them for the summer. Who knew how he would react?

"This is *so* exciting," Grace yelled running in circles. "Maybe it was a pirate's gun." She stopped running to lean over him. Kell now sat on the ground peering at the gun in his lap."

"Is it dangerous?" she asked.

"I don't think so, it's too rusty," he replied. He looked through the chambers and saw there were no bullets. The trigger didn't seem to work either. The gun felt heavy in his hand and bits of rust crumbled onto his palm. Then he noticed initials engraved into the handle. "R.F.M."

"Huh," he mumbled, "Letters on the bottom of this, Gracie."

"Oh," she said, bouncing nearby.

Just then he heard a sound off in the brush. He stopped to look around, but a few seconds passed and he heard nothing but the breeze.

Kell pulled his pant leg up and tried to shove the pistol in his sock, but it was too big.

He could carry it to the cabin in the back of his pants like a detective, but he didn't want the cold, dirty metal against his skin. Plus, even though the gun was empty and probably didn't work, he didn't like to imagine it going off near his gluteus maximus. He set it down to sort out his socks and straighten his pant leg.

"Can I carry it?" Grace asked again, breaking his train of thought.

He looked at it. "I guess so, but don't touch the trigger and stay close. If we see anyone give it to me immediately. Promise?"

She nodded and they headed back toward Grandad's.

As they got close to the cabin, Kell saw that Grandad was out front in the garden. *Now what?* Kell wondered.

"You talk to Grandad. I know where I can hide it," and Grace took off running.

Kell lunged at her but she was already in the trees off the path. He glanced toward Grandad, who was already looking their way. Kell raised his hand in the air with a weak smile and walked toward him. He sighed, *Time to do some gardening.*

7

Kell knew Grace didn't understand the danger of having the gun, likely hadn't thought about it, and almost certainly didn't know what she wanted to do with it.

This was the way his sister always did things. She got an idea into her head and did it whatever the cost.

Kell trotted to the front of the house, where Grandad was kneeling, picking what looked like peas in the garden. He was picking them and eating them straight off the vine while putting some in a bowl. They looked like crunchy worms. Grandad didn't look up as Kell approached.

"Want some help?" Kell asked.

Grandad gave a short grunt that could have meant, well, anything. Kell dared a glance to see what Grace was doing, but couldn't spot her. He knelt down to pick.

"So, these are peas?"

Grandad gave him a dumbfounded look and picked up a small pile of weeds to take to a nearby compost bin. Grace approached, passing him on the way.

Kell glared at her. "It's okay," she whispered. "I hid it."

Grandad returned so all Kell could do was shake his head. He pursed his lips together until their edges were white. Kell was furious, but he also knew his sister. Grace was predictable. She would lead him to it whether she wanted to or not.

Grandad stared at the cut on Kell's elbow.

"Hurt y'self?" he grumbled.

Kell nodded. Two could play the silent game. Grace had escaped back into the coop and was tending to the chickens. There were two.

Grace yelled out, "What are their names?"

"Mooseguts and Knucklehead," Grandad responded.

Grace laughed and chased them around their coop.

The ridiculous names would normally have thrown Kell, but he was busy resisting the urge to go and grab his sister and get answers. He didn't want to draw attention to the situation.

After a deep breath he finally responded, "I fell."

"Gathered that. Where?" the old man pressed.

"Over there," Kell said.

"It's such a nice island, Grandad," Grace beamed as she cooed to one of the chickens tucked in her arms. Her eyes were shining.

"Be more careful next time," Grandad said heading for the house. "Get some kindling for dinner before you come in."

"Where do I find it?" Kell asked, not admitting that he really didn't know what kindling was.

"You don't find it. You chop it," grandad said and pointed to the hatchet near the woodpile.

Kell walked to the hatchet and looked at it where it lay on a chopped piece of firewood. It looked sharp. Was he even old enough to hold it?

Grandad shook his head.

"Pshew."

He walked over, moved Kell to the side, and placed a log on the block, swung through it and two halved pieces fell neatly to the ground on each side. He then chopped them into smaller sticks, gathered them up and put another piece on the block. Grandad stepped back and crossed his arms. Kell picked up the hatchet, raised it, and took an awkward swing. He missed the log altogether and almost hit his foot.

Grandad gave up on him and went to the porch to untie his boots.

Grace continued to dote on the birds, trying to hold and pet them, but she stole frequent glances at her brother. Too frequent. She must have hidden the pistol nearby, but this was no time to ask.

"Yer twitchy," Grandad told her, his thumb running down a suspender. "What's with you?"

She shrugged and looked away.

Grandad gave her a suspicious look but went back to taking off his boots and rubbing Crockpot's ears.

Kell walked near the coop. While Grandad wasn't looking, Kell supplied Gracie with his best nasty look. It wasn't as good as hers, but he needed her to know he meant business.

"I'm going to get more firewood," Grace said. She scampered out of the chicken coop, a look of *Who me?* pasted over her face.

There weren't many places she could have reached in the time she had so it was likely in the coop. He'd have to check later.

"Bring the peas when you come in," was all Grandad said as he walked into the house.

They walked in through the front door. The cabin was one large room and a small kitchen was tucked into the corner near the front porch. The interior didn't feel the same as the rest of the property. It was tidy and well maintained.

Grace began looking around like an excited puppy. She went to the kitchen and pulled back hand-sewn curtains, which hung from below the counter. Behind them Kell could see shelves with four of everything stacked neatly in their places: plates, glasses, and bowls. The sink sat under a window overlooking the rockers on the porch and, beyond them, the garden. The vast waters surrounding the island peeked through the thick trees far off in the distance.

She ran her hand along the small dining table and bounced on a love-seat couch. Nearby was a small woodstove that stood in the center of the room. Grace pretended to warm her hands as she walked past. A metal pipe rose from behind it up to the ceiling. In five steps she was at a small wall that separated, but didn't fully enclose, a neatly made bed in the corner. A framed photo of their grandma and one of their mother sat on the bedside table. The one of Grandma felt to Kell like it didn't belong here. He had only known her from her visits to Portland.

To the left of the door and the woodstove were a long couch, a wooden chair, and a ratty ottoman. The ottoman must have accompanied a cushy chair at some point, but it now sat lonely in the corner. Grace sat on and tested every one.

There were two mattresses in the other corner blocked from view of Grandad's bed by the little wall. They weren't proper beds but single mattresses lying on hand-built two-by-four cots. While Kell stared at the lack of walls around their "bedrooms," Grace scurried over and began to unpack her bag onto one cot. She tossed her few belongings onto the small endtable and into a box under the bed. There was an empty box under the other cot too. Kell went to his bed—as if he had a choice—and sat down.

Grace, her stuffed bear already tucked under the scratchy wool blanket, yelled, "Bye!" and ran outside. He started to yell after her but he stopped himself. The rules at home were specific, home by dark. Besides, he knew she'd stick close after their adventure. He hoped.

"The dog needs feeding," Grandad said looking out the window over the garden.

Knowing he wouldn't get more instructions without the deflating-tire sound effects, Kell searched for anything that looked like dog food. Just inside the door he found a small garbage can with a scoop and food inside.

"How many scoops?" he asked. At first Kell was annoyed at the lack of response, but he looked up to see two fingers on the old man's hand.

He put two scoops into the bowl outside the door. Crockpot let his body fall to the floor near the bowl with a sigh. He looked at the bowl but didn't eat. A long icicle of drool formed from his jowls.

"Well, eat. Isn't that what you want?" Kell asked the dog.

Crockpot continued to stare: at Kell, then the bowl, then back at Kell.

Grace walked in from outside and scratched his neck. "Get it, boy, you can have it now," she murmured and ran her hand down his back. The tip of his tail wagged slowly, but his chin stayed on his front paws.

"The dog is as weird as everything else," Kell muttered. "Tell me where that gun is," he whispered. But she shook her head, "You always get to be the boss. Quit bugging me or I'll tell Grandad." He decided to bide his time and walked away.

Grandad was crumpling paper into a small white stove, another chimney extending from it, near the dining table. He lit it, deftly tossing a few sticks on top of the burning paper. The kindling crackled as the newspaper caught, and the light on Grandad's face went from yellow to a flickering orange. He stood, one hand under a suspender, and tossed a blackened wooden match into the fire. Smoke rose from the growing flames in swirls around his head, and a moment later was whisked up into the metal chimney to mingle amongst the tall trees outside.

Kell took a moment to dig through his bag to find his Ology.

"Awww," Grace groaned, "Do you have to pull that dumb thing out again?"

Grace had many names for his thick 3-ring binder: Borology, Smellology, or *That Dumb Thing* if she couldn't think of anything else. Kell admitted it was difficult to tote around, but he had kept it near since his mother and father had given it to him a couple of years ago.

He had always asked a lot of questions. So many that many adults used words like intrigued, curious, and bothersome to describe him. His parents had joked with him, both being biologists, that he was his own Ology: Kellology. After that, whenever he researched a topic he would place the article in a plastic cover and put it in the three-ring notebook.

Kell looked up "kindling" in a portable dictionary his parents had added. The definition of sticks to start a fire now made sense. He wished his Grandad had explained it. His parents would have. He flipped to "old" in his thesaurus. The binder had a little bit of everything.

old – *adj advanced in age* - elderly, aged, grizzled, hoary, ancient, decrepit, doddering.

For some reason, reading words like "doddering" and "ancient" made him feel better.

An old pendulum clock chimed five chimes. As the fifth chime clanged they heard fingernails scratching on the floorboards and Kell turned in time to witness Crockpot shove his head into his bowl and inhale the pile of dry nuggets in three breaths. The scratched-up bottom of the bowl was licked clean in seconds. The dog wagged his tail as he looked at Kell, then Grace, then Grandad. A burp escaped his lolling, red tongue, and kibble-breath drifted up past Kell's nose. Crockpot's eyes looked back at Kell, then away, then back—eyebrows right along with them—as if to entice Kell to pour a few more bits of food into his bowl. When the new food provider didn't budge, the dog trudged over and sighed as he took a position in the corner near the ottoman.

Kell was directed to shell the peas while Grace set the table. There was to be a fork on the left, knife and spoon on the right, napkin under the fork; the knife and spoon weren't to be on the same side, Grandad soon told her.

Their grandad placed the shelled peas in a small bowl along the few inches of counter space. He carefully measured some spices and placed them into the pots before carefully cleaning off the cutting board. The white enamel stove didn't look as if it would hold one pot, let alone two. Kell noticed that putting kindling into the stove was tricky as well. If the stove got too hot, it would burn the food. But he couldn't put the wood in too slowly, either. The small kindling burned quickly, and would go out if he didn't stock it continually. It was an art to keep it all going. He couldn't imagine how the oven worked.

Kell nicked his thumb while peeling potatoes, and the head chef took over with a grumble. His hands moved like lightning and in no time four potatoes rolled naked at the bottom of the sink. Kell attempted to do the last two faster but kept nicking his fingernails.

"I'm bleeding," he said as he headed to the couch to recover. Grace moved to the ottoman to pet Crockpot.

"Wash your hands, then mix the dough," Grandad said to Kell before he could sit down. Kell followed the directions on a recipe card tacked to the wall. Only when the biscuits were baking was Kell finally allowed to rest.

When smells of fresh-baked biscuits wafted from the oven Grandad announced, "Time t'eat."

On cue, Grace sat down. She pushed Kell's Ology, which he had set on the table, out of the way and grabbed her knife and fork like a hungry medieval queen.

"Mmm," she said after she had taken a bite. Kell had to admit it was good. Fresh garden peas with buttery mashed potatoes, homemade bread, and chicken that melted in his mouth. Kell usually hated peas, but these were actually pretty tasty. They didn't squish like the thawed frozen ones that they used at home, but crunched in his mouth. He wondered what was for dessert.

They ate and cleaned up. Grace finished clearing the table. Dishes had to be stacked precariously on the edge of the small counter next to the sink to be dried and put away immediately.

After dinner Kell lay down on the couch to read. During the school year at home he always did his homework right after school, so later in the evening was his time to do as he pleased. He looked forward to it more than any other time of day because he could read books of his choice.

He reached back to click on an old red lamp just over his shoulder as he nestled into the cushions. First one shoe, then the next thumped to the floor. He flipped the pages of a book on ancient armies and breathed the smell of the pages into his nose.

Crockpot moved to the end of the couch, sat on the floor, and rested his chin on the edge inches from Kell's feet. He stared sideways at Kell.

Kell was just getting lost in a world of Viking ships, when he heard the voice. "Help your sister. It's 6:00."

Kell didn't know why 6:00 was important, but the Viking ship *Gukstad* was about to plunder an island. "But it's my time to read," Kell pleaded. He sunk as low as he could into the pillows. "We always read after dinner." He looked toward Grace for support. She continued to wipe off the table, pretending not to hear. Grace didn't like reading. Kell knew she wouldn't be sad to see that evening tradition disappear.

"I'm going to check on the chickens," Grace offered as she put away the last dish. By the time Grandad opened his mouth to stop her, the door had slammed shut. Kell shook his head.

"I'll go get her," he said in his most helpful voice while marking his page. An old sock full of marbles landed with a whump on his stomach.

"Marbles," Grandad pointed toward the small table.

Kell sighed, "Marbles?"

With his big, wrinkly, calloused hands, Grandad placed an old green board on top of a flimsy card table. "Yep."

Kell read one last sentence as he let each leg thud to the floor. With Kell's legs no longer on the couch, Crockpot jumped up and curled into a tight ball right where Kell's feet had been.

Kell plunked down in the chair at the table and put his head into his hands. He glanced back to see Crockpot's eyes willing Kell to stay put.

Grace burst back through the door, her cheeks and the tip of her nose rosy from the cool evening air.

Kell motioned to the chair, "Looks like no reading tonight."

She brightened and plopped herself into the available chair.

"So what are marbles?" Kell asked.

"Round. Made o' glass. They roll." Grandad retorted.

Grace looked at her brother and smiled. She didn't always understand jokes at her brother's expense but she certainly enjoyed them.

"I know what marbles are," he said. "Is it a game?"

Grace started to sort the cloudy green marbles from the shiny red ones.

Grandad stopped, and studied Kell's face. He didn't seem angry or happy, just as if he were observing something that he didn't quite understand. After a few moments he returned to setting up. Grace's hand looked small next to the old man's as she scooped up a die and tossed it across the board. "Six," she exclaimed.

"You're out with that," Grandad said.

They looked at him and the board but neither moved.

"Pshew, never played? What's your mom doing to you?" His voice got quieter as he spoke the sentence.

Actually talking to me and teaching me things, Kell thought to himself. *All you do is make weird sounds with your mouth.*

Both of his parents were great that way. They helped with anything, especially his mom. She always answered any questions or helped find where to look if she didn't know. Even kids from their neighborhood sometimes came by their house when they needed help with homework.

"You need a one or six to start," the old man explained. Move your color around the board until you get them home. You can knock other players' men back. Can't pass your own man. First player home wins. Exact roll gets 'em in. Roll to see who goes first."

On the board paint of various colors was smeared in each recessed half-circle hole. Many were brown, but some looked as if someone tried to match the colors of the marbles. The die bounced across the board, adding to the hundreds of tiny divots in the wood. Kell watched it roll to land on a two.

Kell didn't yet know if anyone whose village was invaded by Vikings ever escaped alive. He had his own predicament to escape before he could find out.

Dice rolled, players moved.

"Gracie," said Grandad, "Been playing this a long time."

Since when does he call her by her nickname? Kell wondered.

"I'd like to be called the Annihilator please," she said with a warm smile. That was one thing about her; Grace's smiles were always genuine.

"Annihilator," he smirked, "This board has been in our family for two generations. I used to play it with my dad and he played it with his dad. Ladyfolk always welcome. Your mom played a mean game of marbles."

She smiled, bigger this time.

"Every night at 6:00 sharp. Hope you'll join me."

It was the first glimpse of warmth that had come from the man, but it wasn't directed at Kell.

"I'd be delighted, kind Sir!" Grace bowed her head. "It's fun."

"How do you know," Kell scolded, but it sounded more like a whine. "We've barely played." She gave him a snotty face.

Since he was already annoyed, Kell threw out a question that had been bothering him.

"Is there plumbing on this island, Grandad? Like with running water and real toilets?"

His smile vanished at Kell's voice.

"Yep," Grandad responded.

"Could you get plumbing?" Kell said.

"Yep," he said as he turned toward the stove.

"Why don't you? It would be more comfortable," Kell said.

"Got a toilet," Grandad said.

Kell rolled the dice. Grace polished her last red shiny marble not yet on the board.

Kell was bored and with that came impatience. He thought of what he'd be doing back home right now. Something *he* wanted to do. Certainly not something an old grump had done his entire life. As his thoughts of home wandered back to the present another question occurred to him.

"Did Grandma play this game with you?" he asked. *She probably had better things to do,* he thought but was smart enough to keep it to himself.

He would have enjoyed himself more if she were by his side at that very moment. But if she had been there, she might also have elbowed him in the ribs to pay more attention to the change in his grandfather's face.

"Your turn, Grace," Kell said.

Grandad continued to stare at the table.

"Grace! Your turn, gah," he whined.

All Kell wanted was to push Crockpot off the couch and open his book. He was mad his sister had hidden the pistol. He wanted to be done with this game. He could feel his temper rising.

"Don't you ever talk about anything? What about Grandma, you haven't even said anything about her. Didn't she live here with you? Did you just play marbles and not talk to her too?"

The words came in a short, loud roar.

"Leave it!" Grandad's bellow rang through the house and into the forest. It was a warning, like the three short blasts a ferry sounds when a sailboat wanders into its path. Not so much volume as depth; as if from his soul.

Kell looked to the floor. After the room quieted again he let his eyes creep upward. Afraid to look directly at the old man's face, he stopped at a top button of his flannel shirt. His heart pounded. Peripherally, Kell could see that Grace's eyes were popped out of their sockets, her mouth agape.

"Sorry," Grandad mumbled, "your roll, Gracie." He got no reaction. "Actually, you two clean up," he grunted. "I'm goin' fishin'," and he was gone.

The bang of the door echoed in Kell's ears. Kell sat dumfounded at the table. The thought that his Grandad was going fishing in the coming darkness and didn't have a fishing pole didn't break through his numbness. "What are we doing here?" he sighed. He put his chin into his hand and dragged his fingertip around on the board.

Grace hopped up and began to put the marbles back into their sock.

"Guess you should have taken a deep breath that time, huh?" she said.

Kell was still sitting at the table as Grace hummed, put the chairs and card table away, and got herself ready for bed.

•

At three in the morning Kell awoke to a scream. He strained his eyes into the darkness and pulled the covers near his nose. As he wiggled his toes for warmth it came again, but this time it sounded more like a screech. *It's just an owl*, he thought. He knew they were nocturnal, ate small rodents. Probably ready to swoop down and nab a mouse at that very moment. Knowing this didn't make it any less terrifying to hear right outside.

He heard a large splash far out in the Sound. The night sounds carried well despite the cabin being inland. Kell knew there was a lot of sea life in the San Juans. He had done some reading before they arrived, but how could a little harbor seal make that much noise? What else was out there in the dark waters?

Kell focused on Grace's familiar breathing, on the dog whimpering in a dream, and was asleep before the owl gave another hoot.

8

Kell opened his eyes and saw the miserable little cabin walls surrounding him. He dragged himself out of bed and noticed everyone was already up and gone. How could Grandad leave them alone? They were just kids. He walked to the table and stood looking down at a list that lay on its surface. "Sweep, heat water, and stock kindling," it said. He shook his head.

Kell picked up the list and noticed more writing on the other side: "Get eggs, feed Crockpot, Moose and Knucklehead, water garden, put dishes away. Restock TP."

"You've got to be kidding me," Kell said. One day and he already felt he could order them around by a note? *What about breakfast?*

Grace ran in yelling, "Look Kell! Look what I got!" In her hand, buzzing around in his face, was a small, off-white, speckled egg.

He took it from her and turned it over in his hand. It was still warm.

"I got it from a real nest, Kell. I went into the chicken place. I squeezed through the hole and found it. I wonder if there's more. I'm going to go see," and she was off again. She was in a full run by the time she was across the room. She looked up too late to see Grandad in the doorframe. She crashed into him, her head bouncing off his belly. The morning sunlight just coming over the trees highlighted the little hairs coming out of his ears. She stepped back, looked up, smiled, and darted around him.

"Chores done?" he asked. Grace had already wriggled through the door, so it was left to Kell to respond.

"What chore do I do first? What do I do after?" Kell asked.

Grandad looked perplexed, "After chores? Do what you want."

"Where's the broom?" he asked.

Grace squeezed back through the crowded doorway with a load of kindling in her arms, which she dropped carefully into the woodbin next to the stove. "No more eggs, bummer," she said and left the room again.

"Pshew," Grandad shook his head at Kell. "Take notes from your sister."

They finally ate after Grandad spent some time in the kitchen. Grandad called it "mush." It was something between oatmeal and papier-mâché. Kell was still trying to figure out which chore to do first and decided he needed to write out a schedule. He took out his Ology and created a table with the list of chores and the order in which he might try them.

Grace slurped down her mush and went to the outhouse to take care of her "business," as Grandad called it. His belly full, the dishes back in their place, and light in the sky, Kell felt his courage begin to return. He ventured outside to stretch his legs. He felt the cool morning air fill his nostrils. It enlivened the skin on his arms and legs.

Grace returned from the chicken coop, not the outhouse after all. Kell had a strong suspician what she had been out to see. Grandad was watching, so Kell let her pass to go back inside.

"If your chores are done you can go to town," Grandad said from the doorway. Kell nodded, though he didn't know how the chores had become his and Grace's so quickly. He also wondered what the so-called "town" might look like. He thought of asking if the old guy even knew what a real town was. He was sure there had to be buildings bigger than an outhouse and a shack. There should be a library at least.

"Can I go?" Grace bounced and clasped her hands at her chest.

"Of course," he answered, as if it were a completely unneccessary question.

"What's to see in town?" Kell mumbled to no one in particular. He resisted the urge to put air quotes around the word "town." He had his fill of Grandad's temper.

Grace yelled at her brother, "Probably only everything!"

Grandad looked at Kell, grunted, "See for yerself. Or don't." He walked to Grace and knelt down to her. They had a short, muffled conversation. His arm was around her as he pushed her toward her coat. "Just stay out of Dead Man's Cove," was all Kell caught.

Kell watched as the old man shuffled across the porch toward the garden. He moved faster than it seemed he should be able to. Just before a tall row of peas he turned and yelled, "Be home by dinner." By the time the words reached Kell's ears Grandad had disappeared behind the wall of green.

When Grace had asked if she could head out on her own, Kell had expected the normal adult response. At the very least would be the standard questions and demands: Where are you going? Who are you going with? When will you be back? Call if you're going to be late. Likely they would be shorter versions since Grandad didn't use many words, but the idea would remain the same. Grandad was their guardian for the summer. It was his job.

Kell was certain he'd at least be asked to go with her, but Grandad was already gone.

"I'll go with you, Gracie." Kell offered as his little sister neared the end of the porch. Her grimace didn't hide her disappointment but he ignored it. *I promised Mom.* This could also be a good chance to grill her about the pistol.

They set out on a trail that led into the woods, away from the water. Soon Kell was looking up into the branches. He occasionally got a glimpse of a creature making one of the many forest sounds, a chipmunk or a tiny flitting bird, but usually he saw only fluttering leaves—an invisible orchestra. They passed through a meadow, dodging hovering butterflies near low shrubs with pink flowers. Some kind of yellow-orange wild berry grew in higher patches. Then the trail meandered back into forest. Shadows were cast down from the trees onto tall ferns. Dew gathered into drops across dark green, waxy leaves. Kell thought it was salal. His father used it as a centerpiece for their dining room table when they had guests over. Grace had run ahead to chase a tiny chipmunk and he came across her crouching at a patch of moss surrounded by ferns, trees, and bushes.

She watched a spider crawling through a miniature tree. Sunlight peeked through branches and lay on the ground in spots like lazy cats. The walls of the tiny clearing were made of plants.

"I'll bet gnomes live here," Grace said.

"Feels like a grotto," Kell said.

"What's a grotto?" she asked.

"Something like a cave," Kell answered.

"Grace's Grotto," she smiled.

With Kell prodding her to leave they continued down the trail. Mysterious rustling sounds came from behind the giant ferns and tree trunks. A couple of times Kell stopped to peer into the growth, but whatever it was quieted when he stopped. It reminded him of trying to find a cricket amongst rocks, except he feared this one was larger and more hairy.

"Quit worrying, Kell, Sheesh," Grace scolded. "You're a scaredy cat," she smirked, and adjusted her underwear. Kell continued to look into the underbrush. As if to prove her point she turned her back on the creepy-sound-filled, dark forest.

No need to be scared, he told himself.

They crested a slight hill and the trail changed to a gravel road. Branches reached for their faces. A few minutes later, they heard the murmur of deep voices. Two shadows approached from around a bend. Kell wasn't sure how he could tell from this distance, but they didn't seem friendly.

9

The distance closed between them and Grace waved with a cheery "Hi."

Two boys, one short and one tall, stopped and stared. Their shoulders were slightly hunched. One chewed a toothpick while the other chewed gum.

Grace's curly brown locks and dimpled smile usually charmed whomever she met. People would ooh and ah and say things like "Adorable" and "Just Darling." The tall one snorted and wiped his nose with his shirtsleeve. A part of Kell was comforted by the boys' reactions. Not everyone fell under her spell. She began to skip in a circle around them all.

The shorter boy with a brown flannel shirt stood facing Kell. The taller, in blue, was nearer to Grace's circular path. Their clothes were limp and well worn. Their noses curved down to identical rounded knobs at the tip. They had dark eyebrows and straight hair. A greasy, white triangle of forehead showed through the brown hair of both. They were matching versions of each other except for their height. They both wore flip-flops.

The tallest one stepped into Grace's path. "Who are you?" he said with a scowl.

She stopped to avoid bumping into him, crossed her arms defiantly, and stared him in the eye.

"I said who are you?" he persisted, moving the toothpick to the opposite corner of his mouth.

"I'm Kell," Kell said finally, realizing that Grace already starting a protest of silence. "That's my sister, Grace."

Grace raised her chin higher and squinted.

The short one turned from Kell and kicked at a good-sized stone with his exposed bare toes. It tumbled across the gravel into the ferns. Kell watched for a grimace of pain, but the boy didn't wince.

After a long moment he snorted and spoke, "I'm Jones. That's Jones," he pointed.

"We're twelve," they said in unison.

Grace giggled. Kell gave her a stern look and she quieted.

"You're staying with your grandad," the taller Jones said. It wasn't a question.

"Yes," Kell nodded, his eyes questioning.

Small Jones just stared. The toothpick voyaged back across his mouth.

"We don't like visitors much," Big Jones said.

"Oh," Kell answered. He wasn't sure what they'd done to deserve this treatment.

"You have weird names," Grace blurted and started up her circle dance, making it bigger to avoid the Jones in her way.

"Not sure we need criminals on the island either," Small Jones added.

Big Jones picked a rock and threw it at a tree. Small Jones did the same.

Kell gave them a perplexed look, "What's that supposed to mean?"

"Let's just say your family tree is a little shaky." Without another word they loped past and continued down the road. They alternated kicking more rocks as they went.

"See you around smugglers," Big Jones yelled without turning around.

After they had gone Kell said, "What was that all about?"

Grace shrugged, "Who cares?" and ran ahead. Kell followed but soon she was around another bend and out of sight.

Smugglers? Shaky family tree? I have a great family. Baffled, he focused on catching up to Grace.

Despite the cool greetings from islanders, he thought he would have felt more stranded on an island, almost claustrophobic. "Surrounded" was part of the definition of "island," after all. But new things peeked out from all around him. The greenery tried to hide the water, but every now and again he would catch a glimmer like the sun breaking out from behind the clouds on an overcast day. The ever-present boulders that pushed up through the grass were sprinkled with lichens and tufts of dry grass.

The trail widened just as a gigantic blue-gray bird drifted across his path. The bird's wings moved as if in slow motion as it headed toward the water. It alighted on a large, bouncy fir branch and began to preen its huge wings. It seemed content. Kell took a deep breath. A higher limb sagged under the weight of a black bird he hadn't noticed before. They looked like two kids bouncing on bunk beds.

Kell turned and headed to another thick gathering of trees. The dirt crunched under his feet. Past the trees was a clearing with three small buildings.

Closest to him was a one-story building with "Post Office" hand-painted in white letters on the door.

Leaning on a pickup with chipped red paint was a slim woman with long, wavy brown hair and a pleasant smile. Grace stood next to her waving her arms around in wide circles. Horn-rimmed glasses sat low on her nose and her arms were crossed. Kell couldn't yet hear them, but Grace looked as if she were telling an epic tale.

Kell walked closer. The post office didn't look large enough for anything, yet Kell peeked through the window and on the inside were thirty or so post-office boxes. It had a front porch with a large window to the right of the door. The hours were posted 10 – 2Pm, the "Pm" capitalized as if trying to become a real word.

There was a two-story building beyond the Post Office with an external wooden staircase running up the left side. On the lower level a few chairs sat empty on a narrow, worn front porch. Above the porch a sign hung from two rusty hooks; it read "Store" in the same white lettering painted on the post office door.

Grace ran toward him and dragged him over to the pickup truck. "This is Bernadette!" she yelled too close to his face. "She is the postwoman, and she's the store owner, *and* she's the librarian – isn't that cool?"

"Hi," Bernadette smiled, "you have a very sweet sister, Kell."

"Hi," he replied. She was pretty. He thought he should say more, but could only manage a nod.

For the next twenty minutes he listened to her on the steps of her store. She had been on the island six years and described some inhabitants of Mobray. Most had been here all their lives. Many lived on the island's southern tip, on the other harbor, so she didn't see them often.

"The postal clerk before me, Miss Midge, had nothing better to do than chat. My first few months running this place people would show up at 5am for coffee or 9:30pm for tea. I made the hours more conventional pretty quickly," she said.

The store hours were from 7:30 am to 4:30 pm. Bernadette had a tendency to read upstairs during open hours, but people could leave their money on the counter or write their total on their account in a ledger. She occasionally received too much and would put the extra money into a jar. If a resident wasn't able to buy all they needed they could pull from that kitty.

"It's my own little non-profit organization," she shrugged.

Kell didn't know what a non-profit was but he didn't care. All he knew was that Bernadette was nice.

"We just met two guys. They were kind of..." he trailed off.

"Weird!" Grace yelled as she bounced in the bed of the pick-up.

Bernadette laughed. Kell caught himself smiling as she brought her eyes back to his.

She nodded, "The Jones Boys? It does take a while to get to know them," she acknowledged.

"I can see why," Kell said.

"They're... eccentric," she said.

If that word means weird it's perfect, Kell thought.

"They don't have an easy life," Bernadette rubbed her neck. He liked to massage his mom's neck when she was tired. He wondered if Bernadette was tired, but blushed at the thought.

"They live with their uncle. He isn't around very much so they often have to take care of themselves. How are you liking your visit so far?" she asked.

"It's okay. Not much to do though." He thought he'd sound more grown up if he complained. *You know... same old thing.*

She laughed. "I have a feeling you'll find a lot to do very soon."

"It's just that I had plans for the summer," he said, surprised he was sharing this with her.

"Plans have a way of changing, don't they? Islands tend to be fascinating places though. This one is no exception."

Kell had trouble paying attention. Bernadette's shoulder strap had slipped down. It slid up her arm then slipped down again as she reached up to adjust her glasses. He did his best to look at her eyes and nod up and down often, but he could feel his face reddening again.

Bernadette had heard about Kell and Grace already. She said that island news travelled fast.

"Let me show you around the store," she flashed her smile again. Kell would have dug her a ten-foot hole that moment, had she needed one, but seeing the store would do. During their tour of the dusty little library, Kell was relieved to see a computer opened to a website. *At least that works*, he thought.

"It's an island, not the dark ages," she said, seeing him light up at the sight of the computer.

"Can I look at a couple books?" he asked.

"It's a library, Kell," she smiled. "I have to catch the mail boat." Bernadette ran off in a flash. "Come visit soon," she yelled behind her. Kell got the feeling she was often busy. She reminded him of his father that way, but her version of busy was better somehow.

He could hear Grace yelling outside, so he sat in the old plastic chair in front of the computer and turned to the screen. At school there were strict rules about getting online without an adult present, but he needed answers. And anyway, what if there were no adults around to help?

He typed "pistol" in the search field and pressed return.

10

That afternoon, Grace fed the chickens while Kell watched. She moved her arm across her body in a beautiful arc, scattering feed across the yard. The chickens scuttled in the dirt around her feet.

"What do we do with the gun, Kell?" she asked as she threw another handful. She looked as if she had done this her entire life.

Kell reached for an egg from a nest inside the coop.

"Forget it, Grace. I don't want to make Grandad mad again, do you? Let's just leave it hidden until I can find out more about who we can trust here."

"But what was the gun for, Kell? What do we do with it?" They were good questions. He was curious himself.

He felt the weight of the three eggs in the basket. Back home when he walked down grocery store aisles with his mom, it was his job to check the dozen refrigerated eggs for cracks. These eggs were still warm and nestled in straw. Jupiter-like swirls of color on their surface. The quiet clucking in the coop comforted him like pattering raindrops on the roof back home.

His pants were getting dirtier here, and it smelled like chicken poop, but he definitely preferred this to a fluorescent-lit store.

When he rummaged through another nest his knuckles bumped into something heavy. It didn't feel like the surrounding warm splintery, old boards. He eased his hand further under and his fingers wrapped around something cool and metallic. His index finger naturally glided into a slot— for the trigger! Great, at least now he knew where it was.

He heard Grace approach and raised his hand to scratch his head, leaving the pistol where it was.

She entered, stared at him for a moment, and went to the feed can. She didn't take her eyes off him and spilled corn all over the floor as she scooped more into her bucket. He acted busy fluffling up the pile of straw like a pillow. She came and stood next to him.

"What are you doing?" he asked with as much innocence as he could muster.

She didn't say anything, but rustled one hand underneath the straw.

"I already got all the eggs. Unless you think chickens lay eggs *under* their nests," he said.

She shot him a glance and left for the chicken yard in a huff. Kell followed her to the porch with the basket.

Grace stopped and turned on the porch.

"Hi," he said as naturally as he could.

"I'll take that," she said. She grabbed the basket and walked back to the coop.

Kell followed her.

Grace took the basket and placed in its normal place near the nests. She returned the feed pail to its hook as well. Kell lingered. She stood near Knucklehead's nest for far too long. When she realized that Kell wasn't going to leave her alone she moved to leave but stopped near the door. He saw her looking up into a dark corner of the coop shed. She put her hands on her hips. Her eyes were smiling. He had seen that look a thousand times. She may as well have been wearing her cape.

"I know where the gun is, dork," he taunted, "you don't have to sneak around anymore. But at least it's safe. Let's just leave it there." She nodded.

"I just don't like it when you get to know *everything*," she whined.

It didn't take her long to recover, and she looked high on the wall. Kell joined her in the shadows and squinted. Just above the height of his head, he saw the rope with the hook on the end. Grace had obviously returned it when she hid the gun. But high above it was a mounted cupboard barely noticeable in the shadows.

"I saw something earlier," Grace grabbed a rickety wooden ladder, leaned it against the wall, and balanced on the first two rungs that creaked and moaned as she climbed. The ladder was patched with extra pieces of wood on a few rungs and looked to be a thousand years old. Kell wondered when ladders had been invented.

He shook his head. Now that she knew where the rope was she would likely use it to climb up or down a tree or a cliff. Something dangerous.

"C'mon, Gracie. Why do you need to go up there?" he asked. He wondered what could be in a cupboard that high on the wall. It was an odd place for a cupboard.

Her bottom continued to wiggle up the ladder.

He pictured her in an arm-breaking plummet toward the floor.

"Let me do it," he pulled at her leg.

She looked down past her feet and rolled her eyes. "Kell, you're just going to get scared."

"Shut up," he said.

She came down. He started up the ladder. The rungs groaned under his weight. On the fifth one he looked down past his untied tennis-shoe lace. The floor was already far below. He turned back up too quickly and lurched, gasping as he swung his arm to regain his balance.

Three minutes later Grace teetered high on the ladder and reached for the cupboard door. As she opened it she extended her other arm in a graceful ballet-like pose.

"Show off," he said.

She looked in the cupboard.

"It has a box in it," she said.

He squinted up and could just make out the shape of it.

"Well, don't bring anything down. It's probably heavy and you may lose your balance."

Before he finished the sentence she was descending with a medium-size cardboard box balanced in one hand. She set it on the floor and stepped back. Through a thick coating of dust they could just make out a large letter "G" written in black marker. Kell opened the lid of the box and found a small leather-bound book with tattered, yellowed paper sticking out the sides. He carefully picked it up. Underneath were a pair of dirty gardening gloves and an old beaded necklace coiled at the bottom. Kell carefully opened the cover of the book. On the first page in strange, curly handwritten script he read:

E. Edgecumbe
1865

"It's a notebook," Grace whispered.

"Gosh, really Grace?" he mocked.

The numbers on the page percolated through Kell's brain as he tried to assign meaning to them.

"Grace, if that date is real, this book was written more than a hundred years ago."

He was in awe. How many old things were going to fall into his lap? A gun and now a journal? Bernadette hadn't been kidding about islands being interesting.

"Whose stuff is this?" Grace asked.

"Well, we found it in Grandad's shed. There is a G on top. Maybe it's Grandad's?" Then Kell realized something. The gardening gloves, the necklace – the G didn't stand for Grandad. The G stood for Gertrude, their grandmother. She had liked gardening, which explained the gloves, and she probably used to wear the necklace. But the question that interested him most was this: Who was Edgecumbe?

11

The next morning, after breakfast, as he had after every meal so far, Grandad cleaned the kitchen.

Despite the moss-covered entryway roofs and the dusty corners of each building, the kitchen was always immaculate. Nothing about the house was in such disrepair that rain would fall on their heads or a wall would fall over, but his attention to detail in the kitchen far exceeded that of other areas of his home.

The dishes were stacked in their spots on thick wooden shelves. Cups were turned upside down in neat rows. Silverware was stacked in slots within a wide flat box. Not in a drawer but on the counter next to the folded knit placemats they used. He finished by hanging the towel, corners carefully matched, across the faucet.

When the kitchen looked that way it also meant he was likely about to "go fishin'."

This morning he put his hands on his lower back, bent back a little, and then headed out. He still didn't carry any gear, but Kell didn't give it too much thought. He had other things on his mind.

Kell had stuffed the journal under his shirt and smuggled it back to the house. He hid it under the mattress until he could find a more secure location.

Grace had made a quick whispered argument that she had been the brave one to fetch it and should therefore hold the journal, but a quick "Are you kidding me?" look silenced her.

After Grandad's feet crunching on gravel faded away and Grace ran outside to play, Kell carefully pulled the journal from its hiding spot and plopped it onto his bed. He kneeled down and hunched over it with his back to the door. He remembered outlaws of the old west having to sit with their backs to the wall, so he angled his body to keep an eye on the door. He wondered if soldiers ever had to do that, too.

The cover was browned on the edges. He turned to the first entry, to more of the old script handwriting. Black splotches of ink were scattered across the page. It read:

English Encampment, 1865
Royal Marines L.I.

"Marines?" he whispered. *Edgecumbe must have been some kind of soldier*, Kell thought. How many wars were going on in the U.S. in 1865? He flipped more tattered pages. Most were brittle with torn edges.

He heard someone tromping onto the front porch. It was likely Grace doing something annoying, but Kell shoved the journal under his pillow just in case. He grabbed his book and pretended to read.

"*Pshew*," came from behind the door.

Kell's heart pounded while the shuffling and sighing continued. What was Grandad doing out there? Untying his boots?

He heard footsteps treading away. After he was sure Grandad had left— Kell peeked to be sure—Kell pulled the journal out and set it carefully on the table. Back in his seat, his hands to each side on the table, he again stared at the date on the front cover. "1865."

"Almost 150 years ago," he whispered.

He tried to think of what was going on 150 years ago. History wasn't his strong suit. He had always found it somewhat boring, but he imagined huge naval battles on foreign seas. *Marines have something to do with the Navy*, he thought. What had he stumbled onto? He turned a few more pages and saw many dates scrawled near short, abrupt entries. The first was in October and said simply: "arrived tusday" followed by "helped dig cistern." It didn't sound like battle, but maybe that would come later. They probably had to set up the camp first.

He didn't want to push his luck and have the journal visible if anyone made another surprise visit, so he hid it away and got to his chores. It was his turn to chop kindling again and he was beginning to enjoy the challenge.

●

Over the next day Kell thought of nothing but the pistol and naval battles. He envisioned the soldier running from behind trees to attack the enemy, or an officer looking dignified on the battlefield or on the deck of a majestic ship.

He also planned out his schedule. Morning was for chores—not his decision, but he was getting used to it—then breakfast, then studying the journal if everyone was out of the house, which hadn't been much lately. Then he could do what he wanted. What he wanted frequently involved filling his Ology. It was getting a lot of use. The section on pistols, war, and the year 1865 were toward the back so casual snoopers both young and old had less chance of finding them.

He had gone to Bernadette's the day before and taken the journal with him, but she was too busy to help him. Her snail-speed internet connection was tied up filing her quarterly business taxes. She said it took the computer's entire focus as well as her own. He wasn't quite up to sharing the journal with her anyway. What if she thought it was best to send it away? He wanted more information first.

Since there wasn't much else he could do without giving away what he had, he was surprised to find that chores were a great way to have time to think. When he did his work Grandad didn't bother him with questioning stares or *pshew*s.

Kell balanced a section of log on top of the chopping block; he had a bit of time to practice. Blisters that had formed on his hand the first day were healing into callouses. His palms gripped the wooden handle. He aimed for the middle and took two slow practice swings. With one swing he dropped the blade into the grain, then picked up the entire hatchet with log and struck again. Two pieces fell on either side of the block, one much larger than the other. They weren't as even as Grandad's but it was progress. Amoeba-shaped patches of sap covered his hands but after a while the pieces turned into a pile. It was satisfying to know his work stood ready to start the fire that cooked their food.

The large birds he had seen earlier were called herons. He continued to visit where he first spotted them as it seemed to be a regular perch. Two were always together and seemed to be mated. Nearby a bald eagle often watched him from the high branch of a snag. Sometimes a large black bird bounced on a tree limb nearby and held its wings open toward the sun while it screeched like an angry old woman. He hadn't seen other birds spread their wings in that way, so he wasn't sure if they it was warming or drying itself, or just showing off.

A little path that Grace had discovered near her mossy grotto led to a rocky beach. On the shoreline, harbor seals would pop their heads up from below the water to watch Grace and him play around on the rocks. Kelp and driftwood were perfect for building pretend cities.

Grace had dirt on her clothes and a smile on her face each and every day. She would disappear for the morning or all afternoon. Sometimes she would tell him what she'd been up to, but most times not. He wasn't sure where she was going, but he figured it was to see Bernadette. He had seen them read books together in the old orange chair at the store while brushing or braiding each other's hair.

One of those days when he stopped by, he had quickly logged onto the computer and googled "San Juan Islands War" on the off chance it would brush up his local military history. He discovered something called "The Pig War," but he didn't have time to go into it too much as he had only come to town to fetch Grace home for dinner. Maybe that was where the pistol was from. Then again he couldn't be sure. It could have been from anywhere.

Maybe Edgecumbe had a pistol? He wished he could remember the initials on the gun he'd found. He would have to look next time he had a chance. And what did those twins mean about his family. *Maybe I'll ask Grandad. Yeah right.*

The place Kell could most count on finding Grace was with the chickens. She would gather eggs from under Mooseguts's and Knucklehead's warm bodies as she whispered and cooed to them. She liked the soft clucking sounds they made as they scraped at the ground. She said it sounded like people laughing from far away. They seemed to like her, too, at least when she threw them feed. She was careful to shut the gate of the coop and instructed Kell to do so as well. She didn't want her sweeties eaten by foxes or raccoons.

He wanted to share these things with his parents. Maybe he'd have to write a letter. His mom had said they wouldn't be able to receive mail but he could deliver them in person when they returned. Whenever that was. He hadn't heard anything yet, but they warned him that communication would be difficult. He just missed them and wanted to know if they were okay.

One morning Grace went out into the forest to gather flowers for the table while Grandad went to the store. Kell had been thinking about how life must have been back during the time of the journal. After chopping the final pieces of kindling for the cooking stove, Kell loaded the wood box. A feeling of urgency for answers came over him. No one was in the house so he went to his bed and shoved his hand under the mattress. He felt the journal's tattered edge and felt relieved. He ran to the chicken shed. He wanted to write down the initials from the pistol in his Ology so he could look around for names that might match them. He shushed the chickens as he shuffled past, went through the door of the shed, and shoved his hand under the nest. He moved his hand to the right and back to the left, then checked under all the other nests. He was sure this was the right shelf. But nothing else was there. The pistol was gone. *Grace.*

12

Kell charged outside to find his sister, the little thief. Not only did she not heed his warnings about being careful with the gun, she continued to behave in her stubborn, thoughtless way. She always did things because she wanted to, even when it could mean serious trouble. He found her a short distance away from the garden collecting little white flowers.

"Grace," he said.

"They're like stars, aren't they? Like little explosions," she said mostly to herself.

Kell stood with fists clenched. His words came out like steam blasts from a bull's nostrils: slow and angry. "Where. Is. It."

Grace lowered herself to the ground and ran her nose through the mini-field of flowers.

"Where is it?" he said again, louder this time. Two nearby crows flew off. If their mother had been there she would have made him take ten deep breaths.

It was the following silence that caused her to turn.

"What do you want, Kell? I'm busy," she said turning back to her field. "Why do you think he's always so mad?" she asked the flowers. "The gun. Where is the gun?" Kell asked.

"Our pistol? I don't know. You have it," she said. "You found my spot, remember?" She glared at him as she said it.

"Tell me where it is right now!" he yelled.

She rocketed to her feet, "I didn't take it!" She looked like a stout dwarf poised for a fight.

"Shh. Not so loud. Just tell me where it is," Kell peered behind them.

His voice was low and calm. "Grace, this is serious. It is a pistol. A gun. It's dangerous and Grandad will probably be furious if he finds out. You know I found out you have to be twenty-one to even have one? We'll be grounded for fifty years." He started pacing, "This isn't a game. Where is it?"

"I don't have it." She looked less confident, almost sad, but Kell didn't notice.

"Right, this is perfect. Why do you do this?" he yelled. "Haven't you learned four thousand times how it is bad to lie? I am so tired of you."

The last glimmer of happiness vanished from her face. Her eyes welled up and a tremble migrated down her chin. She turned to shuffle away, her head heavy.

He could barely hear her muffled voice, "I didn't take it and I'm not lying."

She stumbled over a root, caught herself, and ran down the path.

•

A feeling of stillness overcame him and he stared into the infinite shades of green. His words stung and he knew it. He had never seen such a forlorn look on his sister's face. She looked so hurt; so defeated. She was in trouble so often, but almost seemed to seek it out. She was so confident. Nothing seemed to faze her—at least for long—but now something had. Him.

Upset as Grace was, Kell didn't trust that she could keep herself safe. *And I promised Mom.* Kell looked down the path, but she could be anywhere by now.

He raced to the cabin. She wasn't in the chicken coop or the cabin. He sprinted through the meadow and over the path toward the store. Bernadette wasn't there and neither was Grace. He sat on the steps for a moment to rest, watching an ant carry a piece of leaf and hoping she would emerge from the woods. But she didn't.

There was only one place left to check. The grotto. When he arrived, winded again, it was in shadowy quiet. He wasn't sure if she was there when he passed by earlier, but Grace now sat in the hole of the overturned stump, her arms wrapped around her knees. Kell thought he heard her mutter something "brother" under her breath.

He sat down at the base of a nearby tree. She stopped talking.

A chipmunk skittered to a nearby log and considered the intruders. Kell watched the mammal's whiskers twitch and move on to other business. He turned to find Grace staring at him.

"I'm not a liar," she said.

"I know," he said, meeting her eyes.

"And I didn't take it," she said.

He had never known her to be so quiet, so morose.

"Okay," he whispered, though he still wasn't sure. But it didn't matter. "I'm sorry."

He put his hand out to her and she took it.

13

It was time for a plan. He needed to find out what was going on. Why did the Joneses refer to him as a "smuggler?" They said something about his family. What were two jerks saying that stuff to him for anyway? Did smugglers carry guns?

Kell knew he had to decipher more of the journal and get more information on the gun. Those were the only things he had to go on. He let Grace come to the conclusion that she was an expert snooper, so she should keep an eye out for intruders and potential thieves. Kell looked out the window to see her belly down on the deck hidden behind the napping body of Crockpot, her nose buried in his fur. Her legs were contorted underneath one of the rocking chairs. Kell knew she loved the dog, but his fur smelled like old shoes. *At least she's dedicated.*

Where was the pistol if Grace didn't take it? Would Grandad take it? Kell didn't think the old man would be so sneaky about it. If he found it, he would just confront them and ask where it came from. Then Kell would likely have to do all of their chores forever, and maybe play marbles for the rest of his life.

But if Grandad didn't take it then who did? The shed certainly wasn't locked—ever. And someone was always around. The only time he knew no one had been there the past couple of days was when he went to the store to see Bernadette.

It was unnerving to think someone had searched around the house and rifled through their things.

The old book lay open in front of him. He carefully lifted the corner of the first page and let it fall open. He was about to read something written by a military man in the 1800's. What a strange thought. He would probably have to put it down every so often due to the violence. He was a little nervous—what if there were graphic descriptions of a bloody battle? He had to agree with Grace that he was a bit of a wuss, but this was going to be amazing. He'd push through.

Feb 16   repaired fanse round gardun in lower field.

Feb 19   little work done today.

Repaired fanse? The second line made less sense. Was the author going to write down that he had gone to the bathroom, too? From the outside it appeared mysterious, full of ancient secrets, but now mind-numbing phrases lay across the page like wilted lettuce. Words were misspelled. There were no descriptions. His teacher Mrs. Hoffman would have passed out if he turned in a story in this condition. She would mark it up and hand it right back to him to fix. Reading the journal reminded him of how he felt watching his first R-rated movie at his neighbor Terry's house. He had been so excited, but then hadn't gotten any of the jokes and had found it wasn't that exciting to hear people swear. The entries continued:

Feb 21   harvested winter greens

Feb 22   spring seed supplize arrived

Feb 24   shot rabbit. made a fine suppur

Yawn. Shooting a rabbit was sort of cool, but this was no military exercise. Spring seed? Sheesh. Crockpot yawned and stretched one leg out from the couch. Kell looked off for a moment, rubbed his eyes, and continued.

July 14	Harvested beans –good amount brot in. fine wether
August 27	Planted more peas – hope they grow. Geting late
September 2	Capn Bazalgette ordered another daley round of drills. Extra pay still not here. geting cold

Then things got interesting.

McFarlane dead. my

Someone was dead. Kell's heart pumped a little harder and he glanced over both shoulders. Part of the page was torn and some of the writing below "McFarlane" was missing. This was finally more than a garden harvest. He grabbed his Ology and flipped to some blank notebook paper his mom had added at the back and wrote "McFarlane dead."

He reread his list. It was a start, but what now?

Dead. The word stared at him.

His mother always spoke of baby steps. Take a few and soon you're farther than you think. Take a risk—you won't know anything until you try something out. Try anything. These suggestions seemed especially important when it came to a true mystery like this.

He paged through the rest of the journal, but most of the entries seemed to be about gardening and the weather.

He thought he'd take a walk to clear his head. His feet led him toward the path to town. It was sunny and clear and the temperature was warm and breezy. He took a deep breath of the clean air. If there was an officer involved then there must have been some kind of military operation or group. He hadn't read much about local history. Ship captains would be involved in military operations, would likely own pistols, and maybe even keep journals? He wondered again if the gun had something to do with Edgecumbe. And what if Edgecumbe had something to do with McFarlane's death, and that's why he wrote it in his journal? The initials on the gun might help, but he needed the gun for that. He had to get it back.

He would start with this Pig War idea. Bernadette would be able to help. The name brought weird images to mind. Pig helmets and pigs fighting. Who knew? Weirder things happened. He watched the Nature channel.

Along the way, he saw a sudden movement in the corner of his eye. *Grace off snooping?* As he turned a shape moved behind a large fir tree trunk. He stepped quietly to his left to get a better view. Hands appeared first holding a pair of binoculars and then a head came into view. It was one of the Jones kids. Kell didn't think it odd for him to be looking through binoculars in the woods. There was a lot to see. What was odd was where they were pointed. Directly at his grandad's cabin.

14

"Hey!" **Kell yelled.** "What are you doing?" Fern fronds slapped at his knees as he ran toward the twin. The injustice fueled him with more bravery than he had.

"What does it look like I'm doing?" Jones said with no concern in his voice. He kept the binoculars at his face. It was Small Jones. At least Kell thought it was.

"Spying," Kell said.

Jones said nothing.

"Well, are you?" Kell's irritation and nervousness rose as he neared him.

"I suppose," he said.

What was with him? He didn't look in Kell's direction or change his position. Kell stopped next to him as close as he dared. He imagined the binoculars pointed at Grace with her chickens or through the window during their nightly marble game. He felt as invaded as when he had discovered the pistol missing. What if one of the brothers had taken the pistol? If this guy was spying now, perhaps stealing wasn't beneath him. Maybe it was the boys that cracked the twigs when Kell and Grace were returning from the hole? Maybe they had even seen Grace hide the pistol.

In one motion Kell grabbed the binoculars from Jones's hands and put them to his own eyes.

"You did not just do that," Jones said in a slow, dangerous tone.

Kell expected to feel a punch to the side of his head, but somehow found the courage to stand his ground. He inspected where the boy had been looking. He scanned the forest and saw nothing but shades of blurry green. He glanced from the side of the binoculars into Jones's scowling face. It was a threatening look, but he was relieved not to see a recoiling fist coming his way.

Kell tried not to move his chest as he took a deep breath and exhaled.

"What were you looking at?" Kell demanded again without taking his eyes from the eyepiece. He couldn't believe anyone would say this to the menacing figure. Well, he could believe Grace would say it. He just couldn't believe he had actually done it.

Neither could the confused Jones, who put his hands on top of his head in a kind of calm astonishment. "Look past that small yew in the patch of salal. Then straight up from there. It's on the highest branch of the snag."

"What's a yew?" Kell asked.

"Seriously?"

Kell turned to him with a blank stare. Jones rolled his eyes and pointed toward a small sapling, "That young tree over there, near the maiden fern."

Kell had no idea which fern was a maiden either, but he wasn't about to admit anything else to this intruder.

It took him a moment to locate the snag. He pulled the glasses away from his nose twice, each time spotting the dead tree, but losing it as soon as he put the binoculars back up to his eyes. It was more difficult than it looked.

Finally, the lens wobbled across a nest. His heart skipped a beat. He saw two impressive-looking birds. One flapped its wings elegantly. It seemed to want to take off at first, but then it caught its balance and settled back into the nest. The other was harder to see as it was low in the nest, but it looked to be grooming itself.

The nest was like a huge dead bush that the wind had blown into the top branches. He imagined it would take a construction crane to get it up there. What did they eat? Chickens? Small children? Even from this distance, they looked powerful and sleek. And menacing, but he wasn't frightened. He was in awe.

"Wow," he said, his anger shelved for a moment. "What are they?"

"Ospreys. They nest here every year," said Jones.

"They're ... cool," Kell said.

"71-inch-wingspan, 23-inch-tall fish-catching specialists. They fly with the fish's head pointing straight ahead for better aerodynamics."

"Smart. I mean the fish carrying thing." Kell couldn't take his eyes off the birds.

"What did you get out of that hole a few days ago?" Jones asked.

"So that was you I heard making noise in the bushes?" He was immediately angry that he had admitted that much. "You *were* spying. On us." Kell's mind raced. If he said any more, he would end up admitting they had found something.

"What did you get?" Jones asked again. He put a hand on the binoculars and tugged, his tone more threatening. Kell didn't let go.

"Why bother asking if you already know," Kell said, as seriously as he could. His stomach fluttered and felt heavy at the same time.

"You're right," a voice said. Kell spun, almost bumping into Big Jones, who towered behind him just inches away.

"We took the pistol," Big Jones said.

"You ... what?" Kell stammered.

"It wasn't yours to begin with," Small Jones added.

"Smuggler," added Big Jones.

"Why do you keep calling me that?" Kell said.

"Because," Big Jones leered, "You're a little Edgecumbe. It's in your blood."

Edgecumbe? Kell released the binoculars and slowly backed away.

"Quit lurking in the forest and mind your own business," Kell wheeled around and strode toward the cabin as fast as he could. He hoped they wouldn't follow. Bernadette would have to wait till later.

15

Kell paced around the cabin, his heart still racing. But as he calmed down he got angry. They took the pistol—no, they *stole* it—from their property. How did they even know it was there? He wasn't sure he wanted to know. And even crazier was that they thought he was related to Edgecumbe. They had just accused him of something, but he had no idea what.

Kell needed to talk to someone, and he knew who. He mustered every bit of courage he could, and headed back to town. The Jones twins were likely guilty of theft, and he wasn't sure what to do about it. He still didn't feel he could confide in his Grandad. His parents were in South America. That left one adult. Today, she was wearing a floral sundress.

"Bernadette, do you know much about guns?" he said, perched on a stool in the store. He thought if he started out vague he could hold onto at least some of his secrets. He wanted to keep the Edgecumbe comments a secret until he learned more. Plus, he was more than a little afraid of the twins.

"Guns? Not much, I'm afraid," she said. She was preoccupied restocking cans of tomato soup.

"Well, what about old guns?"

"Old guns?" she wrinkled her nose up like she had better things to do than read his mind, which no doubt she did. This was harder than he thought.

"Did you say old ones? Grandad is an old one?" Grace yelled. As usual, she had been hanging out with Bernadette. Just then, she was on the front porch watching a spider.

Kell smiled at her mishearing him. He couldn't help but think of "doddering and ancient" from his thesaurus list.

"Old guns are still guns, Kell. Like I said, I don't know much about them," she said as she started dusting shelves.

"What about old guns from old wars?" he asked.

"Kell. Your point please?" she sighed.

"I need to know how to get more information about an item," he said.

He wanted to tell her, but he was a twelve-year-old asking about firearms. What would she think of him?

She nodded, sat down next to him, and put her chin on her hand.

"Researchers use libraries and Internet resources, but I have a feeling you know that. A lot is available online now. You just have to double-check your sources," she said. "I don't want you going online for a free search without me, though. There is a lot of weird stuff out there."

He nodded, pondering who and what to look up when he had the chance. Maybe he could grab time on the computer when she went to the back of the store. "I just need to look into some history," he said.

"Personally, I've always been fond of cemeteries," she offered. "They are steeped with history. They're never busy, and quiet. That won't teach you about old guns, though. Have you been to the island's cemetery yet?"

"I didn't know …" Kell began.

"That we had one? Most places in the world do, even if you can't see them. You should go. Look for the old tree. I like to sit under it sometimes. It's a nice place to reflect."

16

The next day, Kell walked back and forth on the porch. Grace sat in one rocker, Grandad in the other.

"Quit pacing." Grandad snapped—his left eyebrow higher than his right, a grimace on his face.

"Thinking," Kell enjoyed making a one-word reply to the king of short answers. He wore his jacket. Cooler air had moved in.

"Grandad, what do you know about smugglers?" Kell couldn't believe it came out of his mouth.

"Huh?" Grandad grunted. He peered at Kell, "Jones boys?"

Kell nodded.

"Boys'll be boys. Ignore 'em," Grandad said. *How did he know exactly what I was talking about?* Kell thought.

Kell could tell the topic was closed, but he risked one more.

"What about Edgecumbe?" *Why did I say that?*

Grandad held him in his gaze longer than normal. "Enough about it," Grandad uttered. "Fence fixed yet?"

Kell pretended not to hear. It was useful when he didn't understand what the old man was talking about, which happened often since Grandad usually spoke no more than four words at a time. You could barely form a proper sentence with four words.

"Actually, you can," Bernadette had corrected him when he complained to her. "You only need a subject and a verb. 'I read.' That's a sentence." He had told her that wasn't the point. It was the first and probably last time he would be annoyed with her.

"He means the fence on the chicken coop, Kell. Moosie and Knuckle could be hurt if it isn't fixed," said Grace. "A critter could get them," she continued, a concerned look in her eyes.

Grandad's eyes softened, and he stood to go into the house. As he walked by her he placed his hand on her shoulder, creating a semi-circle around her like a compass. He let his hand fall at the last moment before he disappeared into the cabin.

Chicken wire was the furthest thing from Kell's mind. Grace should have known that. Kell had confided in his sister after his run-in with the Joneses. She over-reacted, of course, and wanted to go pick a fight immediately. Bravery and patience didn't live comfortably together in the caped seven-year-old's mind. She had jumped around, waving her fists in the air and bouncing like a video-game boxer.

Grace opened her eyes too wide and bobbled her head at Kell, trying to get him to join her around the corner to form a plan. He did his best to ignore her and finally mouthed for her to knock it off. She wasn't able to read his lips and started to jerk her head around so much it looked like she was having a seizure. He needed to include her soon before she blew everything.

"Kell, we have to go get those mean brothers," she said in a loud whisper when Grandad was finally, but barely, out of earshot. "They need to pay."

"I know, Grace, but like I keep saying, we can't go sneaking around without knowing more," he said.

Grace's face went sour. Kell walked off the porch toward the garden and around to the chicken coop. He wanted to be well away from Grandad before discussing any more with her. He waved her over with his own perfect "c'mon" head motion. *Way better than hers*, he thought. She stood up, whistled a nonsensical tune, her hands in her pockets. She broadcast "I'm doing something, but don't look at me" all the way across the yard, which Kell thought was pointless anyway since Grandad had just stepped inside.

He yanked her behind the coop, "Mellow out."

She gave her best full-toothed, cheesy smile.

"How about checking out a cemetery with me?" he asked.

"Ooh," she nodded vigorously. "You mean an old and creepy cemetery?" She hunched her shoulders and wiggled all her fingers. She looked like a miniature evil witch, only cuter with no warts.

"Bwah ha haah," she ran around and pulled her cape from under her shirt and whipped it over her head.

Kell glanced nervously at the porch. Grandad was back outside in the rocker, Crockpot's nose bulldozed into Grandad's thigh. Grandad shook his head at the noise across the yard, but didn't stop patting Crockpot's head. Kell thought he saw a smirk, but the man returned his gaze to fallen pine needles near the house.

"You can't wear your cape," Kell whispered.

She froze and hunched her shoulders, this time with dramatic sadness. He imagined what she would look like with a wart on her nose.

"Kell! You need her!" she whined. Kell tilted his head to the left to try and protect his already aching eardrums.

"She could save us from nasty skeletons and gulls."

"It's ghouls, Weirdo, and we can't have The Annihilator. She's too loud. We need stealth for this mission. She would mess it all up. You don't want to mess up our investigation, do you?"

"No," she admitted.

"If you're going to come you have to do what I say," he commanded, trying his best parent voice.

She jutted out her jaw and strutted. "The Annihilator does not take orders."

"I figured you'd say that."

Kell ran over to her, tackled her, and pulled her to the ground. He got her on her back. He put his knees by her ears and trapped her arms under his shins as she laughed and cried out at the same time.

"No cape," he said, digging his fingers into her ribs. She erupted with giggles and writhed like a worm on a hook, but struggled to keep a frown on her face.

"I'll be good," she gasped, "No cape at the cemetery!" she laughed. Grandad appeared, leaned against the coop, and crossed his arms.

"Cemetery?" he asked.

Kell cleared his throat and in the bravest voice he could muster answered, "The cemetery, yes."

Kell expected eyebrows to furrow, but he saw a look pass over Grandad's face he hadn't seen before. It was a mixture of concern and sadness, but it passed in an instant.

He said nothing as the kids stood, brushed themselves off, and walked into the woods.

As they headed away from him they discussed the pistol. Where had it come from? What did the initials stand for?

"The Annihilator is going to solve it," she announced after some discussion.

They went through the meadow and the grotto, so Grace could say hello to her gnomes. Kell noticed she had invented homes and paths where they walked. There was a spot where a small forest of ferns lay beneath vine maples; a world of browns and dark greens dappled with light. She claimed that was the gnome children's playground.

They neared town and Kell reminded her of the importance of their mission. She immediately crouched low, moving like a prowler. He ran across the clearing between the post office and the store, ducking when he saw Bernadette move to the post office steps. He knew she would have helped had they asked, but she might have wanted to come along and Kell wasn't ready for questions.

This was as far as Kell had been past town. When he mentioned that fact to Grace she gave a baffled, "Really?" Who knew where she had been on her solo escapades.

As they went up a gradual rise, a sprawling tree came into view. Branches curved out from the burly, gnarled trunk like arms stretching after a long nap. Other trees surrounded the area but this one dwarfed them all. He thought it was a maple, from the gigantic fat points—"lobes," he remembered—of its leaves. It had obviously been there a very long time.

As beautiful as the tree was, the cemetery was less welcoming. When they crested the hill the light dimmed. It was peaceful, but moody. Dark green moss draped from the lower branches. A low white fence tried to surround it, but had gaps as if it weren't quite up to the job.

Rustling noises came from all sides. Kell tried to look brave but noticed he was staying too close behind the strutting, capeless superhero in front of him. Her confidence was comforting.

A few uneven rows of gravestones crusted with moss and lichen were dappled across the hillside. Each stone had a river of cracks running across its face. A few were toppled onto their backs like helpless turtles. One near him had tumbled onto its face – the engraved name muffled in the dirt.

He ran his hand across one while walking through a row. It emanated cold dampness into the surrounding air. He gasped when a bird exploded from nearby underbrush. Grace looked back at him with a smug expression on her face. Kell scrunched his face in disgust that she had seen him, but was determined to keep his wits. He forced himself to remember that the darkness and shadows were just that. *Think like a scientist*, he told himself. *Just the facts.* He focused on breathing in and out, and began to read names and dates. Some were worn and hard to read. A large spider crept across one, but he read out loud "Margaret Noosam died 1912," which seemed to help. Next to her was "Henry Melon – died 1973." These were once walking and talking humans.

"R – I – P," Grace spelled. "Riip," Grace's voice hummed in his ear like an annoying mosquito breaking his concentration, "Riiiiip."

"It's not a word, Einstein," he mumbled, "It stands for Rest in Peace." His eyes darted back and forth to the dark trees on either side. Another spider skittered up a line of web running above his head.

Grace thumbed her nose at him, "I don't care what it stands for, RIP is a fun word. Fun to say, *riiiip.*"

She trotted around him in a circle clapping her hands together. "I could rest here, too. It's nice."

All of these names had once belonged to living people. Some were even his age. Now they lay in the dark, musty earth. He thought of the old rhyme, *The worms crawl in, the worms crawl out. ...*

Thoughts of being buried took his mind to the pistol, which had also been deep in the earth. Someone had put it into a hole, time had gone by, and now it was a rusty piece of history.

If Kell went to Bernadette's, took a library book and put it in down a deep hole and left it there for one hundred years, it would become a piece of history, too. But people were buried because of tradition. Kell didn't know for sure, but the ritual of burying the dead must have gone back thousands of years. It's just what most humans did, as far as he knew. *Who buries a pistol? And why?*

Someone had been trying to hide something.

It was no surprise that his sister wasn't bothered, but the cemetery felt dark enough without the thought that they were standing on top of dead people. He traced his finger around the characters on one grave marker.

Grace began chanting, "The same, they're the same, they are the saaaame."

"Be quiet. Just for one second," Kell pleaded. What could they be hiding, he wondered to himself.

"Theeese are the same," she sang.

"For the last time, Grace, I'm trying to think. Do I have to define a secret mission for you *again?*" But Kell wondered what she was rambling on about. It was rare for her to bug him about something over and over unless she knew he'd be interested. She knew he'd bark at her otherwise.

"Same as what, Grace?"

She pointed at a headstone. "Same as the book," she said.

He sighed, "Just a second." It was probably a waste of time, and he wasn't sure what she was talking about, but he walked over to inspect the stone. Dead moss partially covered tiny engravings. He brushed dark, organic material away. The headstone nearest to him read "Nancy Edgecumbe died in 1881 a dedicated wife and mother." Below her name it noted the marker was placed "by her loving husband and daughters." Next to the headstone was one with a name that he recognized immediately.

Edward Edgecumbe
R.M.L.I.

b. February 14, 1846
d. January 14, 1890

Kell stood with his mouth half open. "Grace. The journal," he said.

"Really?" she mocked, her hands on her cheeks.

He ignored her. The man who had the journal was buried on Mobray Island? He didn't know how there could be two people with the same name on such a small island. It had to be him.

"I'm bored, let's go," she grunted.

The grave marker made it so real. There was a body under the earth and his hand had written words Kell was now reading. He supposed he had read things written by dead people before, but this was different. This was close to home, and to the island, and to him. Right under his feet.

He had to be reasonable, too. How many Edgecumbes wrote a journal in 1865? The journal was dated 1865 and this man died in 1890. The years matched up. If he was buried on Mobray, Edgecumbe likely lived here on the island, too. It was the same man. He was sure of it. His Grandma had grown up here, too. Maybe Kell was related to this man.

"It's gotta be him," Kell said aloud to test the theory, more for himself than his enthusiastic audience. His head was abuzz.

Something else felt strange. Grace wasn't bouncing. He turned to see her standing over another headstone with a serious look that didn't fit her face.

"Gracie, what is it?" he asked.

She was probably tired, and he was worrying too much. She didn't answer at first. He was about to return to his own thoughts when she spoke.

"Kell, it's Grandma. She's right here."

•

He hadn't ever really considered where she was. His Grandma was just gone. She didn't come visit them in Portland anymore. She was in that unreal place where people go when they are no longer at the other end of the phone. But this was where her body actually *lay*.

"Dead." That was the word their father had first used two years ago. "Your grandma is dead," he had said without much emotion. He had patted Kell twice on the shoulder.

Kell knew what death was, of course, but until he had seen his mother slumped in the corner of the sofa staring out the window, he hadn't understood what it actually meant. For weeks she didn't appear to eat or sleep. Grace would go to her and curl up in her lap. She had wandered about the house at all hours, barely able to make tea. Only after a long time did she talk to them—not just toward them—and then she had taken them into her bed with her and hugged them desperately. She said how much she loved them. It had been traumatic for Kell to see his mother so hurt. Grace didn't remember much, she had been too young. Now, here was Kell's fun, nice grandma who played hide-and-seek with him and brought him a knick-knack every visit, interesting agates, a twisted carved stick, something from the island.

The ground surrounding the headstone was well-tended with orange Gerber daisies.

Gertrude "Gerty" Stepler
Beloved wife & mother

b. July 21, 1924
d. January 14, 2009

Their mom had traveled to Mobray Island to bury her, while they had remained in school. It was one of the few times in the past few years that their father had been alone with them. The only thing Kell was sure of was that it wasn't because Dad wanted to spend quality time with them. He and Grace had mostly stayed in their rooms and played quietly, sharing favorite memories of their grandma.

Gertrude Stepler, Grandma Gerty, had been a regular visitor to Portland. The house had an extra room high in the attic. It was reserved for visiting guests and family, but they called it "grandma's room." A couple of old photos of Grandma's parents were hung on the wall. Kell and Grace had agreed they were unnerving, with eyes that followed you across the room. Grace at age two had said they were "scawy" after wailing like a siren and sobbing at the first sight of them. "They are my parents and I loved them," Grandma had patiently explained. After a long talk about how they could look scary but not actually be scary in real life, they walked slowly up the stairs again hand in hand. Grace gave a repeat performance. The pictures disappeared after Grandma had died.

It wasn't ever clear to Kell why Grandma had always come to them and they hadn't gone to Mobray.

"It's a difficult journey with small children," their mother had said.

Their father, who was much more blunt, simply told them their Grandad wasn't much into leaving the island and had never met the kids so he just never bothered. And their mother never seemed to want to visit the island. It didn't matter. They loved their Grandma and were happy to have her.

About her husband she would smile and say, "Oh, he's just an old grump."

Grace and Grandma used to practice the alphabet together. Grandma would write out her name, "Gertrude," and they would spell Grace's name right below. Grace had only been a toddler and couldn't read, but loved the time with her.

She would sneak them sugar-coated cereal. When their mom left for the lab they would eat two bowls each while watching coveted cartoons. "Screen time" didn't exist with Grandma as it did with their mother and father. Not that they needed it. They were outside on fun adventures around town with Grandma more than they were inside looking at the television.

Here she is. Kell sat under the large tree and looked around. He could tell Grace was beyond bored. She dragged a stick along the ground at the far edge of the enclosure near another gnarled tree, one much smaller than the big maple he sat under.

He couldn't help but compare his grandma's marker to the Edgecumbe stone a few feet away. Edgecumbe's entire family appeared to be buried nearby. A woman—his wife?—and a young child who had lived only four years. There were other families whose members were gathered near one another as well.

He wondered how many people had sat under this tree remembering their loved ones. Had Edgecumbe sat here when his child had died?

Kell had to admit he hadn't thought of Grandma much since they had been here. He didn't associate this place with her. She was his Portland grandmother. She had just been absent for a while. Grace was even further removed, as she had been only four when Grandma died.

Now she was under the dirt beneath their feet. The engraved name was a link to the past.

He meandered among the headstones a bit longer, down a path that led away from the cemetery, and came to a sign:

DANGER
Dead End
Dead Man's Cove

Tall green plants lined the path ahead, closing in from both sides. *Perfect*, he thought to himself, and tried to turn around before Grace saw him near such a temptation. To Kell, Dead End signs were just that—dead. There was nothing to do but turn around. To Grace they meant adventure. It was too late. She walked up, considered the sign for a second, and sprinted past him.

"Grace, it's a dead end," he yelled.

She disappeared into the stand of tall green plants. He heard footfalls, then shouting.

"Ow. Ouch. Ouch! Aaaah!" she screamed.

He ran, and as he did he felt small, sharp stings along his arms. It seemed to happen each time he hit one of the tall, flowering plants.

"Ow!" he yelled, now understanding why she was yelping in pain.

"Ouch! Kell, you have to see this!" she yelled. He entered a small clearing. Grace was sitting on a rock at the base of the far trees, rubbing her shins. Grace had worn shorts, and there were little red raised bumps all over her legs.

"It serves you right, Grace. What are you doing? Jeez. Those things hurt. The sign says Danger. Danger means," Kell stopped short, "Whoa!"

He had come to a steep cliff. He stood next to her and squeezed her shoulder as they watched small rhythmic waves splash against jutting rocks far below. Wind blew over the bay from the north. Near tall-standing old pilings, two harbor seals popped their heads up from the water to look around. With a splash they were gone, sending ripples into old timbers that looked like they had supported a dock long ago. The beach extended around the cove but faded into a sheer rock face on either end.

"Wow," was all Grace could manage to say. Kell noted her legs must have hurt more than she let on; otherwise she would have been picking her way down to the water already. The steep descent would require care, and she would likely fall into the water and drown, but she would surely have tried.

"We need to go," he said. He still felt strange about seeing his grandmother's name on a stone with other dead people. He had the journal on his mind and wanted to examine the entries more closely. And he wanted Grace away from this cove that looked like it lived up to its name. "C'mon."

"Awww," Grace whined.

"Let's just go, Gracie," he urged. "You have sores all over your legs."

The promise of a Marble game, seeing Crockpot and the chickens was enough to lure her onto the path.

They took the trail back but were careful not to touch the tall green plants. Kell looked more closely and saw tiny hairs on the stems. As they headed past the cemetery he looked toward the Edgecumbe stone again. He pictured the date on the cover of the journal. This involved the pistol. He felt it in his bones.

17

"That's why they're called stinging nettles," Grandad said. "Told you not to go."

"Maybe you should watch her more closely." Kell insisted, "She's only a little kid." He didn't often come to his sister's defense but this time he made an exception.

Grace sneered at her brother. Grandad didn't respond, but continued rubbing white paste on Grace's wounds.

"People have died in that cove. Don't go near it," he said firmly.

Grace's eyes widened. "Why did the others go in?"

Grandad frowned at her.

Kell thought it an obnoxious question that would have driven his mom nuts, but he was hungry for answers.

"Doesn't matter. Just stay out of there," he said.

She scratched a spot on her arm, then on her leg. He brushed her hand aside and rubbed in more lotion. She reached to the other leg, receiving the same response. Scratch, brush, squirt, rub. Scratch, brush, squirt, rub.

18

The next day Kell got more time to himself for research. After Grace's wrestling match with the nettles, she said she was going to spend the day at Bernadette's to help around the store or sort mail. Kell knew she was hoping for a story or two in the orange chair. Lately she had been raving about a book of local Native American folktales. Something about Seagull stealing the sunlight from humans and Raven, the good guy, punishing him to get it back. It had her so riled up she hurled rocks at any seagull they came across. Bernadette even complained about reading it to her because Grace would get so angry.

Kell waited for Grandad to "go fishin'" and then settled in at the table to spend time looking at the journal more closely.

Feb 1   Finished gravel path, unloaded barge. Men did wel.

Feb 9   tended beets, started building the officers cabins up on the shelf

If Edgecumbe lived and had been buried on Mobray, as the cemetery led him to believe, it seemed from the entries that he had started out somewhere else. Wherever that was, they had been setting up for something.

Officers' cabins meant that they had intended to stay there for a while, and again seemed to point to something military. Edgecumbe described guns and ammunition being loaded and unloaded, gardening and building, ditches being dug. Though the entries were short and uninteresting alone, Kell came to see them as pieces of a puzzle. He began to put the small, seemingly unrelated details together to form a larger picture.

Awgust 23   horseraces were grand today. Went to Camp San Juan to use Americans pasturs

San Juan? And if Edgecumbe spoke of Americans as if they were "other" people, then he likely wouldn't be one himself. Kell recognized that strategy from logic puzzles at school. Edgecumbe wrote the journal in English; what countries of the world spoke English? Ireland, England, Australia? Hmm.

Nothing much happened through the following autumn and winter, but in early 1866 something else changed.

March 3   McFarlene servis today

That name McFarlane again. After McFarlane died the entries stopped, and didn't start up again until May, when new things began to happen—things that felt different.

May 13   Traded cooper for potatoes
May 15   homested act past – pepl talkin abowt land
May 22   found bote, time for jurney

There had been other periods of time when Edgecumbe hadn't written for a few days, but he always seemed to enter some mundane thing that happened during the same week. It didn't fit his pattern not to write anything for two months. And what did he need with a boat? *Assuming*, Kell thought, *that's what 'bote' means.*

The person who wrote this down was planning something. But then the journal entries went back to the same boring house and garden notes through June and July.

June 10   Brot peas in.
June 13   Hoed the garden today. Fine wether.
June 22   bilt south wall and dug privy pit
July 3   planted tree near kove

There were fewer references to military-sounding things—no ammunition or other men or wartime vocabulary. Kell also noticed a couple other things, which he added to a list of observations he'd started:

Someone named "Cooper" traded something for potatoes.
Edgecumbe went on a "jurney" somewhere new. Was it Mobray? Likely.

And the word "kove." What did he mean by that? He had obviously written that entry after he had moved to Mobray (if that's indeed where he had moved). It likely meant cove, but if he meant a cove on Mobray, was it Dead Man's Cove? Were there other coves on the island?

Something else occurred to him. Why did Edgecumbe even write McFarlane's name down? To write it meant he was important, at least to Edgecumbe, either a friend or a foe.

Kell had a lot of questions, but he was making progress. *Baby steps, just like Mom says.*

With projects at home he often started with the encyclopedia, either online or at the library. Bernadatte had a decent printed one, though it was old. He had to start somewhere and decided to focus on something he could actually look up.

He flipped a couple of pages back through his old notes. His list of his first few days on the island contained notes about the smelly dog, the barrel and pistol, ferns, and endless water.

He laughed at his earlier scared self and looked outside. A breeze blew. The birdcalls, once annoying, he now began to recognize. Crockpot thumped his tail on the crooked porch planks as if responding to his change in mood.

On a whim he flipped through his dictionary. He found "P" for pistol. The definition was "handgun."

"Thanks," he muttered. He loved it when a dictionary stated the obvious.

He could look up "captain," and it would likely be what he thought: a military officer somewhere below a general. He skimmed his memory of other words from the journal. Friend? No. Horse race? Another word popped into his head. He turned to the page with the bold keyword "**bar-en**" at the top of the page, and skimmed down until he found the word he was looking for:

barrel – a large, bulging cylindrical container of sturdy construction traditionally made from wooden staves and wooden or metal hoops. The term is also a unit of volume measure, specifically 31 gallons of a fermented or distilled beverage, or 42 gallons of a petroleum product. According to the 1st-century-ad Roman historian Pliny the Elder, the ancient craft of barrel making, also called cooperage, was invented by the inhabitants of the Alpine valleys.

Cooperage. It was just coincidental enough to catch his eye. He turned to the Cs.

"Cooperage – a cooper's business or premises."

"Are you kidding me?" he said aloud. He wished there was a way to tell the dictionary to quit being ridiculous. He turned back a page. "Cooper - a maker or repairer of casks and barrels."

Barrels, he thought, *I know where there is a barrel.*

19

Kell pondered the earlier journal entries while Grace counted what looked like oyster shells on her bed. Cooper had been in Edgecumbe's journal and traded him a barrel for potatoes. Kell had assumed it was a man named Cooper. Was Edgecumbe instead referring to a craftsman? He supposed a cooper was like a blacksmith or carpenter. Could the barrel from the pit have been the same that Edgecumbe had brought to Mobray? Highly unlikely, but what else did he have to go on? He needed to follow this lead. He reread his notes until his head started to swim. It was all becoming overwhelming.

Maybe, Kell wondered, a barrel would have a special marking if it were from the army? He could go find the pieces and search it for inscriptions. When he and Grace had broken it apart they hadn't paid attention to anything but what was inside.

Kell started talking out loud.

"I know this guy was probably military and moved to this island. His name was Edgecumbe." *Brainstorm, Kell*, he thought. *Nothing is off limits or too silly or stupid.* "He planted things to eat, he might have brought the barrel with the pistol in it, but I'm not sure about that. I'm not sure about anything really."

He turned to Grace. "Would you do something for me?" She nodded eagerly. "I want to check the pieces of the barrel for any words. Can you do that?" He paused for effect. *"Carefully?"* Do you remember where the barrel is?"

"Yeah. Right by the hole you fell in."

Kell continued rambling out loud as she jumped up to leave. "Plus, he wrote things like 'cove' and maybe that's our cove, and about this guy named McFarlane."

"A cove?" she asked.

He nodded. "Yes, but I don't know what it means, and we aren't supposed to go back there anyway. But what if Edgecumbe spent time there? Maybe there's something there that *he* buried. I don't know. I did learn that during the Pig War local boats stopped by on the way to San Juan Island smuggling whiskey, arms, or gold to both camps. Maybe that's why the Jones' were talking about smugglers. The steep cliff walls on each side keep it secluded – it's a perfect hideout. ..."

"You mean like for treasure?"

"Grace, don't be ridiculous. Of course not buried treasure. Just go look for that barrel for me," he repeated, trying to stay focused on things they could accomplish.

Grace ran off, a huge smile on her face.

"Look for a piece of wood with writing on it!" he yelled after her, but she was gone.

•

Bernadette sat directly across the table. Kell twiddled his thumbs. It was a trick his teacher had taught him for when he was nervous or needed to pass time. "It gets you out of your head," she had said. Twiddling in reverse was more difficult so he tried that.

Bernadette inspected her fingernails. After two minutes of silence she tilted her head like an inquisitive dog. A strand of hair dangled down beside one ear, making her even more beautiful than usual.

"Kell, I'm happy to help you with whatever is on your mind but I can't just sit here. I have work to do."

"I have something," he said finally.

"Yes?" she rested her chin on her hand, leaning her elbow against the tabletop. Kell continued to twiddle.

She stood up and started to sort mail.

"It's a secret. You can't tell anyone," he said.

"No I *can't* tell anyone. You haven't told me anything," she said.

As she hovered from post box to post box, he took the journal from under his shirt and placed it on the table. She set the mail on the ledge, sat down, and leaned over the book. She read the cover, her upper body creeping over it like a panther sniffing its next meal. Her chin was back on her hand, while her other arm stretched out in front. As she turned the pages, her hand went to her forehead where she flipped her bangs back and forth in her fingers.

"Kell, this is unbelievable," she said.

"We found a pistol too but it's gone now," he said.

"A what?" She looked up.

"A pistol. You know, a gun," Kell answered.

"I know what a pistol is, Kell. So that's what your cryptic questions were about. You've told your Grandad about this of course?" She went back to the journal.

He hoped she wouldn't notice his lack of an answer.

"Where did you find this? And did you say you didn't know where the pistol was?" Her fingers trailed down a page as she spoke.

"I don't know ... around. We just came across them." He knew he shouldn't have shown her. Now he was going to have to tell her everything.

Kell turned the journal back toward himself to look at the pages.

Grace burst in, panting and shouting as she ran through the door, "Look what I found, Kell!" She handed Kell a piece of the barrel. The letters "RMLI" were barely visible in the wood. It was easy to miss if you weren't looking for it.

"Do you like our old book, Bernadette?" She leaned against Bernadette's arm, rested her hands and head on Bernadette's shoulder.

"It's a great book, Gracie. I may have an idea where it came from. Can I see that, Kell?"

She took the board from him. "'Royal Marines Light Infantry.' Where did you get this?"

"Kell found it when he fell in the big hole!" Grace said.

"The big hole?" she asked, a concerned look on her face. Kell gave Grace a stern look for sharing too much.

Bernadette shook her head. "You two are something else. You know that? I think you have discovered some artifacts from a war here, Lady and Gentleman. The Pig War."

Grace looked confused. "Pig War?"

Bernadette nodded. Grace pushed the point of her nose upward, and started snorting in Bernadette's face. Bernadette grimaced at the view up Grace's nose and nudged her toward the door by the forehead.

"Are you going to let me read to you again today?" she asked Grace. Grace nodded as she ran outside.

Kell was annoyed. He wanted to get serious about his research and didn't want Grace interrupting. He took a deep breath and got back on topic.

"You think the journal is from The Pig War, too?" he asked. "He seems to be a soldier, but all he does is list the things he does every day on his farm. And what's the Homestead Act anyway?"

"The American government gave land to people who proved they could take good care of it," she answered, "and this journal is more than that and I think you know it. You better start looking into some San Juan Island history." She paced excitedly. "Kell, this is an important historical document and you need to take good care of it. People will be very excited you've found this."

"Bernadette, I don't want to get in trouble. Can we not tell him about the gun *or* the journal?"

"I don't see why secrecy is necessary, Kell. He's an understanding man." He couldn't believe she would consider Grandad to be reasonable. "Yeah, right."

"I don't like hiding things from people." She paused. "You need to tell him."

Kell had known it would come to this. He thought of the hidden, now lost, pistol and what kind of trouble that was likely to bring. "Yeah. But not for a little while."

Bernadette took a moment and smoothed her dress over her legs. "How long is a little while?"

"A few days? Just so I have time to find more out. It would be better to go to him with more information, don't you think? I was hoping you would help me," he pleaded.

He tried to make sad eyes, but not lay it on too thick. It always worked for Grace.

She looked into his eyes as if they were an honesty meter.

"Oh, I don't see how a few days can hurt." *Thanks Grace*, he thought. "As long as you promise you'll show your Grandad." She grabbed his shoulders. "*Soon.*"

Kell nodded vigorously.

"And I am going to help." Her hands remained on his shoulders. If he had been a dog he would have wagged his tail.

"I'll mark some things I think are more important and we can start there? And I want to keep the journal here for safekeeping. Agreed?" she said.

"What about the pistol?" Kell asked.

"You said you don't know where it is."

"I think the Jones took it, but I can't prove it yet," Kell said.

"Well, let's not start making accusations yet. A gun, really?" she repeated.

Kell nodded. "It was old and rusty."

She looked thoughtful. "You found them in the same place?"

"No," he said.

Bernadette again became distracted reading journal entries. From behind them came strange panting sounds. Kell looked outside and saw Grace wielding an imaginary sword, hacking through a swarm of invisible enemies. She seemed to hold a shield, as well, protecting herself from who knows what kind of counterattack.

"Die pigs!" she screamed. "Yaaaaargh!" And she charged into the mob, managing to giggle and look fighting mad at the same time.

"Pigs?" Kell asked aloud.

Bernadette broke from her trance. "Yes, I think her imagination has taken over."

"I don't get it," he said. "Did this war really involve a smelly farm animal?"

"As I said, it looks like someone has some research to do," Bernadette chided and turned to watch the little soldier elbow an unfortunate swine. "And I think Grace might need more accurate information, too," Bernadette added.

Grace enjoyed her fight, battering snouts and snorting bodies, but little did her brother and Bernadette know the real battle was about to begin.

20

When Kell woke up Grace was already gone. She often left on an adventure in early morning, but she usually returned for breakfast. Kell finishd his mush, cleared the table, and headed out. Grace had remained disturbingly quiet on the issue of the missing gun, and he knew she was dying for revenge. Kell had a bad feeling he knew where she was.

He walked along the path and as he neared what he thought was the twins' cabin he heard a male voice yell, "Hey, what are you doing?"

Oh no, what has she done? He found a hiding place between two large trees and heard the yelling turn to screams.

He peered through the trunks to see the two brothers lying down on the trail with their feet raised in the air. Big Jones crawled to Small Jones and started to look over his feet. He appeared to be attempting to pull something from the bottom of his big toe. When he did so his brother writhed in agony. Kell couldn't tell but he thought there was blood all over the bottoms of both of their feet.

Grace appeared on the hillside above him—a look of panic on her face. To her left was a large ravine with fallen logs and briars. To her right was a hill with underbrush. The brush was thick, and she seemed unable to decide where to go.

Kell watched her turn around, crouch, and watch as the brothers began to crawl toward her. Big Jones yelped when he accidentally hit an injured foot on a stick. Small Jones put his hand in a piece of something on the trail and stopped to shake it out. They weren't going anywhere fast but they were moving.

Kell stepped from behind the trees and waved at her. She made her way through the brush toward him, but snagged her shirt on a stiff limb and stopped to unhook it. She finally reached Kell with wide eyes and a smile mixed with terror and excitement.

"Hey!" a yell came from behind them.

Her big brother took her hand and they ran.

21

"What have you done?" Kell asked his sister as they reached the luckily empty cabin and blew through the door.

"Gracie? Answer me. You could have been hurt. You were gone and I kind of knew where you went and then they were coming." He couldn't stop talking. "You scared me!"

She laid the pistol in its oilcloth on the table. Then stood back and put her hands on her hips.

"What were you thinking?" he asked.

"They took our gun," she stated, not an ounce of regret in her voice. "I got it back."

"Yeah, but. ... What happened to them anyway?" His eyebrows rose in amusement.

She grinned. "Oyster shells. They're really sharp when you smash them up. Eggshells don't work as well. I tried them first."

"Wow," he said. "Wow." *The folktale from Bernadette's.*

"Now I know why Seagull gave the sunlight back when Raven did it to him," she said with obvious pride. "Those things really hurt."

As the adrenaline wore off their smiles grew until they started to giggle. "They were lying there with their feet in the air, they looked like dead bugs," Kell laughed. He realized he hadn't laughed—really laughed—since they had arrived and soon he was lying helpless on the floor.

Kell caught himself when he saw the pistol on the dining room table. "We should get out of here," he said suddenly. He put the pistol and sack deep in a corner shelf in the kitchen behind some pots he had never seen his Grandad use.

Since Grandad wasn't around they went to Bernadette's. Kell thought they should be near an adult in case the Joneses came looking for vengeance. He hoped they had a couple of days while the boys' wounds healed, but he didn't want to take any chances.

●

"You keep talking about a Pig War," Grace dug right in as they settled in to browse materials Bernadette had set out for them. "Pigs are nice. Why would they fight?"

"That's not what she's talking about, Grace," Kell said, although he was still a little mystified himself. He picked up a brochure and began to read.

Grace continued with her train of thought. "Helpers at the petting zoo say that pigs are smart and clean. What's it say, Kell?" she asked. She leaned onto his shoulder and smelled of bubble gum. Bernadette had given her a piece from the counter jar and was now outside watering some flowers.

"Let's see. It looks like an American farmer named Lyman Cutlar shot and killed a pig owned by a British company. The farmer said the pig was eating his potatoes." "What kind of a name is Lyman?" Grace wanted to know.

"I don't know, hush," Kell answered. "The two countries had been fighting over who owned the Oregon Country for a long time already. Oregon Country was what is now Washington, Oregon, Idaho, Montana, Wyoming, and British Columbia."

94

"Get to the pigs," Grace smacked her gum as she spoke. She started to bend his earlobe back and forth to watch it wobble.

"They finally broke it along the 49th parallel on June 15, 1846. The English got the northern part, and America got the southern," Kell continued. Flick, wobble. "Stop it," he swatted her hand away.

"Pair of lells? What are lells?" Grace asked.

Flick, wobble.

"Shh. One thing they couldn't agree on was who should get the San Juan Islands. Armed forces came from both countries to protect what they thought was theirs. For twelve years they each set up camp on San Juan Island as if it was already theirs."

"Sounds like kids at school running to get a computer during rainy-day recess," said Grace. "Mrs. Gem always makes them go back to their seats and be last."

Flick, wobble.

Kell stood up to avoid his sister. "It seems like that's kind of what happened. Some German guy named Kaiser decided for them in the end."

"Kaiser? Like the rolls we get for sandwiches," Grace observed.

Kell stared at her for a moment. "Anyway, it looks like he basically helped them decide."

"Did Kaiser Roll flip a coin or do rock, paper, scissors or something?" Grace asked.

Kell didn't answer. He was confused.

"I thought a war was, like, war," he said to no one in particular. Bernadette had gone to sort mail in the other building. For a war, it sounded awfully peaceful. "Where were the guns and battles? The blood? Did they all just grow gardens and write in their journals?"

He found a dictionary and flipped to war.

"War – a state of armed conflict between different nations or states or different groups within a nation or state."

"So if you're armed don't you have to actually use the gun to call it a war? Huh," he grunted.

"Poor pig. He didn't do anything. He was probably just hungry," Grace said, her lower lip stuck out for effect. "The countries just argued?" she said.

"Guess so." He scratched his chin.

"So they both lived on the island?" she asked.

He nodded. "Not this one. It says they were on San Juan Island."

Kell flipped through pages. Grace blew air from her mouth to try and get her lips to vibrate. Bernadette returned and replaced two books on their shelves.

Grace suddenly lit up with a thought. "Maybe it's like when we both want the cushy chair at home." She smiled at the memory. "You dive for it first then I squish in with you."

"Yeah, I don't even like to go to the bathroom because that means you'll get the chair," Kell said. "Then Mom brings us popcorn. That's a great example, Grace," he admitted.

Grace beamed. Kell noticed she turned away but held a proud grin on her face.

"I don't like it when your boney butt pushes into my side though," Kell smiled.

Bernadette joined the conversation. "What motivates you to sit in that chair?"

"It's the best spot," they said in unison.

"That's what both sides in the Pig War thought," she said. "The San Juan Islands had good land for settling and raw materials."

"What are raw materials?" Grace asked.

"Wood for houses, grain for bread, whatever it is that both sides want or need for their society. Something that helps them survive or grow. In your case it seems to be popcorn," Bernadette answered.

Kell added, "That seems silly to argue over a little island."

"All arguments are silly to someone," Bernadette said, straightening the books on a shelf.

Grace's face darkened. "It should be called The Silly War! They sound just like stubborn bratty kids who won't share their toys." She sheathed her imaginary sword and started doing a weird dance with a goofy face. No need to defeat pigs after all.

So the Americans and English both thought they were entitled to the islands. They both camped out on San Juan, refusing to leave.

"They were both on different ends of the same island?" Kell asked.

Bernadette nodded.

"That reminds me," he said suddenly. "Where's that journal?" Bernadette handed it to him. He flipped through until he came to a page that had baffled him. Now it made more sense:

August 23   horseraces were grand today. Went to Camp San Juan to
                use Americans pasturs

"So if Edgecumbe was a soldier in the English Army would he ever visit American Camp?"

"He could have, but whether or not he did I don't know," she said. Kell went back to some information he had found on a website earlier.

It turned out the soldiers were bored, didn't have much pay, and often had no family with them. They were forced to do hard work. The site described how many of the soldiers became friends and went to each other's camps for dances and friendly competition during the twelve-year occupation.

Kell was baffled. "I don't understand. How is it a war if the opposing sides are friends?"

"War is complicated," she said. "Plus, 'war' is just a word. Sometimes a word can't capture all the nuances of a situation."

"I still don't get how during a battle people can be friends. I've never heard of that." But a light bulb went on. What friends didn't fight? All friends had arguments. He and his neighborhood friend, James, had fights over their video games or the street nerf football game all the time. But he knew James. What if you didn't even know the other side—the enemy? What then? If someone came in and took an island that you thought was yours, you'd just think they were evil. The Jones brothers took—no, *stole*—the pistol. That was evil and they most certainly did a bad thing. Did that mean he and Grace had to go to war with them? He supposed they already had, since Grace launched The Revenge of the Raven campaign or whatever she now called it. They had struck first though. They deserved it. This was getting confusing.

"Perhaps not during an actual battle. But The Pig War didn't have any of those. History is fascinating, isn't it, Kell?" she said.

"What does history mean, *exactly?*" Kell asked.

"It's the study of what humans have done in the past," she replied.

"I'm going to study bugs," he said. "Humans make no sense."

"Neither do you," a gruff voice sounded from the doorway.

They could only see the figure in silhouette, but there was just enough light to make out suspenders hanging from his shoulders, and Kell was certain the shadows above the eyes were a bit hairy.

The shadow raised a hand, "What's the meaning of this?" Dangling from his finger was a familiar rusty pistol.

22

After the scene at the store, Bernadette apologized profusely. She said it was her fault and spoke to their grandfather for a long time out of earshot, her hands gesturing like overexcited butterflies. They walked home with the pistol and journal tucked safely under Grandad's arm.

Once back at the cabin they all entered and Grandad walked to his room with the pistol and journal. He returned to the main room empty-handed, making no effort to conceal where he put them.

Back home lying meant a good grounding or at the very least losing video screen time. Here they had discovered and hidden a firearm, and taken what was likely a valuable historical document and not told anyone, but their Grandad didn't do *anything*. He just went on about his business cooking, cleaning, tending to the garden, and 'goin' fishin'.' It was horrible. Kell felt like a mouse scurrying on the ground watching a hungry hawk perched high on a limb. Since being found out, he had yet to feel the hawk's talons sink into his sides. Maybe the hawk was going to make him dig a new outhouse pit or something.

Kell started to relax. He knew relaxing wasn't a good idea. Grandad didn't look as if he was thinking about them hiding the pistol from him; it was hard to keep his guard up. Waiting for a punishment was far worse than getting one.

After a while Grace and Grandad were sitting in the rockers. Grace had Crockpot's nose in her lap and was rubbing his eyebrows. She had just cleaned out the chicken enclosure—shoveled the yard, washed off the roosts, and swept out the entire coop.

"Y'do good work." Grandad nodded without looking at her. Kell overheard him from inside and felt an urge to speak up about all the good work he had done. He wanted to start listing things, but could tell he was going to whine and thought better of it.

"My great-great grandad built this place. Did it all," Grandad said as they walked into the room. "No books, no computer. Just muscle." Crockpot padded in behind him and sat near Kell's feet. Grandad placed a few more sticks on the cooking fire for lunch, his flannel shirt hanging out in back.

After stoking the fire, he returned to the kitchen to lay out bread for sandwiches. Some homemade soup simmered on the stove.

"Gotta get to fixin' that outhouse," he said, letting out a short grumble-sigh.

Grandad had mentioned the broken board in the outhouse floor before. How it needed to be done to "keep the critters out." It was on the edge of what Grandad seemed to view as important work. It wasn't cleaning the kitchen, so he didn't feel it needed to be done immediately. But it also wasn't straightening mis-hung cedar siding on the outside of the cabin, which was never repaired. It was somewhere in the middle, so it remained to be fixed, but he talked about it often.

Kell tried to keep quiet. Maybe The Annihilator's get-away-with-anything attitude was rubbing off on him. Their dad had always told him that Grace could pull it off better than he could. "Stick with your strengths, son," he suggested.

But he said it anyway. "Who would ever want to work on a thing as gross as an outhouse?" It came out sounding snobbier than he intended.

His vocal chords vibrated, sending the sound waves across the room to wiggle into those wizened, hairy, old ear canals. The second they reached their target they pushed a button in the old man's brain. The electric pulse sent a message to his face muscles, which pointed the fuzzy caterpillar eyebrows down at a harsh angle toward the bridge of his nose. The nose then pushed the corners of his mouth crooked. Everything on his face scrunched toward the middle of his face and created an impressive scowl. The realization came too late to Kell that this would have been a really good time to keep his mouth shut.

It wasn't hard to predict what was coming next.

•

Now his head was down the toilet. He looked up past his armpit to beautiful blue sky framed by the toilet seat. He was certain spiders were licking their chops waiting to crawl into his ears. He reached upward—or downward, depending on how you thought of it—toward the small pile of nails on top of the seat, trying his hardest not to drop them down into the pit.

Grandad had thought it very important to replace the board under the seat as well as the one on top. Kell wondered if there had even been a board there before, but he wasn't going to ask. This was pretty insulting already. As he extended one hand toward the corner, the hammer he held in his other hand slid in his grip a couple of centimeters. He clenched it at the last second. He envisioned it slipping from his hand into the dark, germ-infested goo below. He could just see going to Grandad and pleading.

"Grandad, the hammer is in the poo."

"It's not gonna come up itself," he'd say. Actually, he wouldn't say anything. His eyebrows would shape themselves into a stern, immovable arch, and Kell would have to figure it out on his own. He tightened his grip on the hammer.

Kell lifted himself up and took a moment to catch his breath. The outhouse smelled dank and stale. He walked out the door away from the outhouse and the air, even a few feet away, became more tolerable. Suddenly, the diluted stink jostled a corner of his memory.

He ran the few steps back to the outhouse and looked down the hole past the still-unrepaired board. The hole was a similar diameter and depth. Could it be?

He ran toward the chicken-coop shed to grab a long board, a shovel, and the long, thick rope with the hook Grace had discovered. He would be more prepared for the hole this visit, but he had a new hunch. If he was right, why might someone throw a pistol into the bottom of an outhouse pit?

23

Kell walked away from the shed and quickly past the coop. Mooseguts had pecked Knucklehead until her feathers had fallen out, and Grace was stroking his neck. "Grace, c'mon."

She didn't move right away, but she could never refuse a promise of adventure and Kell looked all business. She left the chicken to fend for herself. As Kell's fast walk turned to a jog, she followed.

"Kell, where are we going?" she asked, breathing heavily.

"Where y'off to?" they heard from behind them.

They both stopped and turned to see Grandad sitting on a stump carving into a piece of wood.

"Um, to see something," Kell replied.

"I'm coming too," Grace yelled. "Grandad, come help us!" She tugged on Grandad's hand.

Kell stared angrily at his sister, but she was facing the other way and didn't see him. Not that it would have mattered. Grandad, wearing his standard flannel, suspenders, and grimace was already putting his knife in his pocket to join them. Kell didn't move as they walked toward him. He let them pass and turned to follow.

Grace somehow knew right where he was headed, and raced on toward the hole. When Kell saw that Grandad was really coming, he hesitated. He wasn't used to his Grandad being part of things.

When they arrived, Grace was already lowering herself on the branch they had left.

"Wait," Kell yelled, now annoyed that he hadn't just done all this himself.

Grandad sat on yet another stump and pulled the knife and wood carving from his pocket. He put the carving down next to him and began to clean under his fingernails with the knife blade. Kell had witnessed this once before. He had hoped he wouldn't have to again.

Kell tried to focus on what he had come to do in the first place. He looked down and made a mental note. The hole looked to be about the same depth as Grandad's outhouse, and the ground around it was flat enough for a building to stand above it. The mostly deteriorated boards that had collapsed during his fall seemed to be all the same length—perhaps the walls of an outhouse. So far it fit his theory. This was an outhouse pit.

Grace had climbed back out to look at Grandad's carving. Kell picked up the rope and tied it to the board. He placed the board across the hole and sat at the edge intending to lower himself down.

"Grace, help me," he said as he leaned over to try to get some of his weight onto the rope. The board slipped across the top of the hole toward him, and his feet slipped deeper into the pit. His stomach lurched. "Step on the board to keep it steady," he pleaded, his voice filled with panic.

A part of Kell knew that he didn't *need* to go into the hole again. Everything down there was still dirt and it wasn't going to prove anything further. But a bigger part of him needed to go down the hole. He needed to prove to himself that he could.

There was a distinct feeling of nothingness beneath him as he wiggled his bottom backwards to its original position. He was terrified. Until his weight was supported from above there was risk of the board pulling sideways, but in order for that to happen he had to thrust himself into the hole and trust that the board would hold him. He had to sit and breathe for a moment.

"I don't need to go down," he thought aloud. "I have what I need."

"Pshew."

Blood rushed to Kell's face in embarrassment as he turned to eye his Grandad. He didn't need to go down. He was certain this was what he thought it was, an old outhouse pit, but Grandad made fun of him and he was tired of it all.

"What's your problem?" he yelled.

A look of shock spread across the old man's face. "Don't have one," he said. "Not sure why I'm even here."

"Well, then why are you?" Kell snapped.

"Dunno why. Why you got to be such a grump?" Grandad said, turning to leave.

"At least I talk! I have friends. You don't even visit anyone! Can't you even see your own daughter?" Kell was madder than he'd been in a long time and it was all coming out. It felt good to let the anger rise up.

He heard a scream.

They both spun ready to come to Grace's aid. She stood with her fists clenched at her sides with her face growing red.

"Be nice!" she yelled. "Why can't you both just be nice?"

She turned and ran off into the forest. The sounds of her little body bursting through brush and snapping branches underfoot faded away. The silence that descended was thick and oppressive. Kell and Grandad looked at everything but each other. Kell got to his feet.

Grandad broke the silence first.

"Finish the outhouse. Hunt yer ghosts after chores." He hitched up his pants, tossed the whittled wood into the ferns, and headed back toward the house.

24

Kell sank the last nail into the outhouse board. It felt solid when he tested it, and despite his mood it felt good to see the job done. He supposed he hadn't been himself since coming to the island. He was angry and hadn't wanted to come here. But he was doing better now. He did his chores, his Ology was full, and he was solving a mystery. His Grandad was the difficult one. Grace had no reason to be mad at *him*. Kell shook his head. It didn't matter. She always did her own thing anyway. He didn't have time to think about that.

Grace hadn't come back yet, but he didn't feel like going out to look for her. Grandad was in the kitchen, probably re-stacking the breakfast dishes. Where was it quiet? Where could he think? He smiled. He grabbed his Ology and headed to the house of the crescent moon.

Bernadette had wondered whether or not an outhouse hole could last one hundred years. Kell had thought about it and suggested that maybe the large rocks lining the sides made it harder for it to fall in on itself. She agreed that perhaps that could keep it around so long. *The toilet that lasted a century.* Kell smiled to himself.

He pulled open the wooden door, let the rusted spring slam the door shut behind him, locked it with the rusty hook, and sat on the circular seat. It didn't smell so bad when you were confident no one would bother you. Enough sun peeked through the slits for him to look over his notes and review the story.

An English soldier had been involved in a war. The war consisted of two armies occupying the same island to be sure the other didn't get the land. They participated in what sounded more like summer camp: games, horseback riding, and target practice. They were in a beautiful place, but they were bored, and poor. Two soldiers came to know one another. Edgecumbe and McFarlane. One died. Then Edgecumbe left the army, moved to Mobray Island, and claimed land to start a farm and a family. After he arrived, he buried a pistol in an outhouse pit.

The story sounded pretty good so far, but it still wasn't finished. He tried to remember the rest of his conversation with Bernadette a couple of days earlier.

•

"Why is it an important war?" Kell had asked. "Sure, it's interesting, but c'mon they didn't do anything." They were sitting on the steps of the store.

"That was the big deal," Bernadette replied.

"They didn't fight. That's not a war."

"Sometimes not fighting is more difficult than fighting," she said.

"Huh?" Kell looked puzzled.

"What is something that Grace has done that really made you mad? I mean fighting mad?"

He looked at Grace who was playing nearby and thought about it for a minute. "She busted up a lego castle I had worked on for weeks. She said she was practicing her human hurricane," Kell remembered. It still made him mad to think about. He had designed turrets, a moat, and everything.

"What did you do about it?" she asked.

"Pushed her over. She hit her head on the tile counter corner," he remembered the scene. Grace's head had a huge lump and his mom was furious. She had called their dad at work so he could help come up with a worthy punishment.

"Why didn't you talk to her before pushing her?" Bernadette continued.

"Because I was mad. I had spent days on that thing. It was the coolest thing I had ever built."

"See what I mean? It's easier for kids to throw a fist or yell first. And for most adults, too, though they likely wouldn't admit it to you. Talking about it in the heat of the moment is hard."

She sipped water from a nearby glass. "The attitude back then in northern America was to grab land while you could, and the islands were appealing. America and England were involved in this war for over twelve years. Forty, if you want to count the dispute over Oregon Country. It was like having a big tasty brownie on a plate in a room with two hungry kids. What do you think the chances are of them coming to blows?"

"Does it have nuts?" Kell asked.

"What? No."

"Pretty good then," Kell said.

"So over twelve years, if I remember right, there were about sixteen changes in leadership and small fights between individuals coming up all the time. Considering that the two countries had rather large egos, and there were a lot of unpredictable people with tempers around, that's pretty impressive."

"So they kept talking even when they were annoyed and angry?" Kell asked.

"Steaming mad sometimes." Bernadette nodded her head.

"I hate Georgie McKracken at school. I don't wanna ever talk to him," Grace interjected.

"Try sometime," Bernadette suggested.

She shook her head, "Don't want to." She smiled and waved her arms around her like an out-of-control windmill.

Bernadette squeezed her. "Most people don't, Goofy. That's why we have wars with guns instead of just arguments. But," Bernadette continued, "if you two are stuck together in that big chair in your house and the movie is playing, do you keep poking each other?"

"No, we wouldn't be able to watch the movie if we did," Kell answered.

"Right. So if you were stuck on an island with a bunch of other people and you had low pay, hard work, and none of your friends or family around, would you rather shoot at each other or race horses and have dances?"

•

Kell decided to send away for a list of soldiers who served in the Pig War. He would ask Bernadette for help. He needed to know if Edgecumbe was there. Maybe McFarlane had served with Edgecumbe or was at least on the island at the same time.

The stink from below broke his concentration. It was time for a change of scenery.

25

After **Bernadette helped Kell** send the letter off to the U.S. Army Center for Military History, he returned to the cabin. Grandad was sitting in a porch rocker. It dawned on him that he had never seen his grandfather choose the one on the right, always the left. Kell returned the tools from his outhouse repair to the shed. He replaced them on their marked hooks on the pegboard and stared at the hanging tools until he noticed he had been staring a while.

While still in the shed he heard the porch boards creak. He peeked around the door to see where the old man was headed. Grandad patted Crockpot on the head, walked off the porch and down the path. Kell thought he might as well head to town to talk with Bernadette anyway, so he looked out once more and followed. But when Grandad reached the store and passed it, Kell followed. Soon he found himself not walking, but creeping.

As he followed he realized he didn't know much about his Grandad. This was his mother's father, yet the man was still a mystery, even after living with him for weeks. Usually, when Grandad left the cabin, Kell felt relieved. It meant he could work on things he didn't want to share with his grandfather anyway.

A ways down the trail and well out of sight of the store, the old man pulled off the trail behind some of the tall pink-flowered shrubs and unzipped his pants. He started to pee.

Already surprised, Kell heard something that completely baffled him. It was his grandad's deep voice, not the usual grumble, but … a melody? He couldn't be sure, but it sounded like—no, it was—singing.

I met a little elf man once
Down where the lilies blow
I asked him why he was so small
And why he did not grow

He slightly frowned
and with his eye
he looked me through and through
I'm just as big for me said he
as you are big for you

Kell had to keep looking from behind the thick tree he was hiding behind to be sure the voice matched up with the man. The song lilted up and down, soft and lively. It was quite good. He peeked around the other side of the tree to catch a glimpse of his Grandad zipping back up, doing a quick jig, and then starting to walk again. The grimace Kell had grown accustomed to had disappeared, and Grandad's bushy eyebrows were raised high. He swung his arms as high as his head.

Who was this man? Kell watched him bounce in time with the tune as he passed over the packed dirt and kicked a rock. As Grandad approached a fence, Kell slowed to duck behind a large boulder. It was the fence of the cemetery. The singing stopped. Kell watched as Grandad kneeled near a grave, picking long strands of grass and tossing them to the side.

Kell took care to avoid sticks and dry leaves as he moved closer. Grandad began to talk.

The old man's hands were animated and he spoke as if he was addressing an audience, yet his focus remained on one grave. He gestered, stood up, sat back down again, and continued talking. It was more words than Kell had ever seen him speak. Kell stared for a few moments until he was startled when, without a sound, Grace crept up next to him. He was annoyed and half expected her to be obnoxious—to shout out or to laugh—but she still had a slightly disgruntled look on her face. She gave him a forced smirk, then settled in to watch. Kell used her shoulder to brace himself as they both leaned against a mossy log. A line of ants crossed the log and chipmunks chirped warnings nearby, but they were each still. Neither of them noticed the moisture seeping into the back of their shirts.

Grandad spoke for a while longer, then sat quietly. He stared at the sky and trees for a time.

Kell remembered riding in the car once with his mom. They came upon a car that was smashed and smoking in the middle of an intersection. It couldn't have happened more than a few seconds before they got there, because other drivers were just getting out of their cars. Mom told him to stay in the car and she went out to help the driver of the little sports car, its front end crushed. The man lay on the asphalt in the middle of the road, his hands over his face. He didn't looked injured, but he moved slowly. He got up a few times, and each time those around him tried to keep him on the ground. He kept getting up and asking for his phone. "I need my phone," was all he would say. Kell had never forgotten the eerie look on his face. That same shocked stare was on Grandad's face right now.

Kell and Grace looked at one another and held a silent conversation with their eyes.

They watched as their Grandad bent over, leaned his head over the rocky surface, and kissed the gravestone. Then he began to weep.

Kell suddenly felt embarrassed. He was seeing something he wasn't meant to see. He dropped his hands to the ground to push back toward the boulder and motioned for Grace to do the same. As he did, a small, dry twig snapped under his weight. Grandad turned and saw them both. His eyes met theirs. A tear hung on his cheek. He didn't move to wipe it away.

•

That evening, Grandad did not acknowledge them. He moved methodically through his dinner routine, peeling potatoes, picking up pots, and shifting food across the counter. The only noticeable difference was a few moments of staring off into the distance.

Grace was outside, moving things around and cleaning out the feed bucket for the third time. Kell, lying on the couch, made his eyes move across the lines of his book.

Finally, the table was laid, food steaming in the center.

Grace ran through the door. She had accidentally slipped in the chicken coop and had chicken manure all over her knees.

Her quiet whines lessened as Grandad made efficient moves to comfort her. He wiped her pants off, cleaned her legs, and consoled her. Kell saw him chuckle once, but it passed quickly. He helped her change into fresh pants. After she was changed and they had settled back down, Grandad sat in front of the kitchen stove, poking at the glowing coals. Not knowing what else to do, Kell and Grace sat down to eat.

They started in on their food but Grandad remained in the kitchen, staring out the window, his place at the table empty.

Grace put her fork down. "We shouldn't have followed you, Grandad," she said.

The fire in the cookstove crackled.

As they ate he moved to stare into the fire, occasionally poking at a log. After dinner they cleaned up, put foil over his plate, and started their bedtime routines. The old man finally moved to his bed, took off his clothes, and got under the covers.

When they were all settled into the darkness, the occasional crackle of an ember was the only sound inside the cabin. Kell heard Grace's breathing deepen and Crockpot's snores lengthen. He thought his Grandad was asleep as well, but as he began to drift off he heard a heavy sigh. Kell put his own pillow over his head and closed his eyes.

26

The next evening Kell returned from the store to Grandad stirring the potatoes on the stove. Kell grabbed some plates for the table. He heard squawking outside. *Grace must have come back to feed the chickens*, he thought. She had been gone all day. The chickens were always noisy so nothing should have seemed out of place, and yet something did. Grace, that's what. Grace was out of place.

He opened the door expecting to see his little sister tossing grain across the pen, but she wasn't there. Maybe she had come and gone? How annoying. It was her turn to set the table.

Grandad spooned food onto their plates. Kell put the silverware down and walked toward the coop to inspect the ground for signs of feed but saw nothing. Inside the chicken-coop shack, the bucket sat empty on the dirt floor.

The birds weren't calling out in excitement; they were calling out because they were hungry. Grace *never* forgot the chickens.

"Grace!" he yelled.

Once back inside the cabin he asked, "Has Grace fed them yet?"

"Nope," his grandad raised his eyes to look directly at him.

"She'll come," assured his grandad, but the look in his eyes wasn't convincing.

"I'm going looking," Kell stated.

Grandad didn't stop him.

While the old man put the hot food back into the pans on the stove, Kell put on his coat. He excused himself and began to walk the trail toward town. He hoped she had just lost track of time in the grotto.

•

In Portland, Grace was often late to get home. She would be lost in thought playing some made-up Annihilator game and Kell, who usually didn't stray far from home, would have to fetch her. Since they had been on Mobray her chores had made her easier to keep track of. Even if she disappeared for large chunks of the day, she was always home for Marbles and had never missed feeding the chickens.

When he arrived at the small green trees of the grotto, he knelt into the trunk hollow where he had found her before. A small pile of pinecones and some peanut shells lay sprinkled at the bottom. Probably a squirrel had found her stash of snacks. That could have happened anytime in the last few weeks.

Kell searched under the vine maples, behind large fir trees, and called her name for several minutes. No Grace. He continued toward town. Nettles, now dried to a crinkly brown, leaned over the trail. He bent over sideways to avoid the deadened stalks and quickened his pace.

He heard motion from up ahead. Jones and Jones hobbled toward him on the path. They had flip-flops on their feet, but they each held a walking stick.

Small Jones winced as he stopped in front of them. "We want the gun back," Big Jones said.

"Not now," Kell said and tried to walk past.

Small Jones stepped in front of him and bumped Kell's chest, stopping him in his tracks.

"We'll get it anyway," Big Jones leered.

"Fine," Kell said, "but not right now. I need to go."

"What you need to do is give it back," Big Jones said, striding toward him. He shoved Kell squarely on the shoulders.

"You stole it in the first place," Kell shouted. Kell glanced left and right, looking for the better path around the boys. But Small Jones flicked his walking stick out, and planted it behind Kell's feet while Big Jones pushed him hard in the chest. Kell dropped backwards, his head snapping back onto the gravel, and in a second they were on top of him.

"You're not even from here," Small Jones hissed in Kell's ear.

"So give it back. You little thief," Big Jones said. They had his arms pinned, pressing his back into the rocks and sticks.

Kell spared a peek at his legs. He was sprawled out flat, but the twins were hunched over, curled half up on either side of him with the soles of their feet facing upward. Big Jones had lost a flip-flop in the scuffle. Kell raised his right leg, then swung his foot down. The edge of Kell's shoe caught Small Jones squarely in the sole of his exposed foot.

Small Jones screamed in agony, letting go of Kell's arm to grasp at his foot. Kell swung a wild punch with his free hand, clouting Big Jones across the bridge of the nose as the larger boy turned to look.

He, too, released his grip.

"I don't have time for this!" he screamed and was up and running. He left the Joneses writhing in the dirt behind him. Without looking back Kell ran down the path toward the store.

•

Bernadette only needed one look at Kell's eyes to grab her jacket. They checked frantically behind the few buildings and in the bed of Bernadette's truck. She took his chin in her hand. "Slow down. Think like Grace," she said.

Kell took a deep breath.

"Let's look at the Jones cabin," she suggested. Kell shook his head and explained what had happened earlier. "They can help anyway," Bernadette insisted.

They found the brothers limping along the road. Bernadette ignored their irked faces and asked if they had seen Grace. They shook their heads then looked at each other, then at Kell. The brothers left them, agreeing to help, and hobbled in the opposite direction to look on the south part of the island and ask a few other locals if they had seen her.

"She's probably fine. She always is," Kell said. Bernadette nodded her head, and placed her hand on Kell's shoulder.

They had looked around most of the inland part of Mobray. The shoreline was all that was left. *What if she went looking for treasure?* Kell thought. He remembered reading the tide tables a few days ago. There was supposed to be an extra high tide coming sometime soon.

The light grew dim as they walked back to town. Grandad was on the steps outside the store. His hat blocked the porch light, so his face was lost in shadow. He stood up at their arrival and slipped his hands under his suspenders.

"Pshew."

He set out off down the path to Dead Man's Cove. Without a word Bernadette and Kell fell in behind him.

27

When they reached the cove, Bernadette saw her first.

"Oh my God," she gasped and put her hands over her mouth. "Grace!" she yelled. "Hang on, Gracie!"

She pointed to a tiny figure in the swirling, frothy darkness until Grandad and Kell saw her, too. Grace was grasping onto what looked like a twig and half of her was under the sloshing, white water.

Kell was paralyzed. He had only known his sister as a confident super-hero. She climbed, leapt, and did what he couldn't. She looked helpless and he didn't know what to do.

Grandad moved fast. "We gotta get her out of there fast. No tellin' how long she's been in it." Grandad lowered himself over the cliff. Kell turned to look at Bernadette.

"The cold, Kell," she explained. "Gracie won't last long in that water."

Kell understood their worry. From his reading he knew local waters were known for fast currents and strong tides. Hundrends of thousands of gallons of seawater moved back and forth with each orbit of the moon. Huge ships with powerful engines paid close attention to the tide tables

119

and wind direction. A barge could use thousands of expensive gallons of fuel working against a strong tide.

Grandad grabbed for a branch, but it gave way under his weight and his feet slipped off the loose rocks below. He crashed roughly onto his side, gouging the right side of his ribs. Kell could see the pain in his face, but Grandad didn't cry out. Bernadette and Kell each took a hand and helped him back to the top.

"I'm going," Kell stated.

"No," Grandad said.

"I'm going," he repeated.

"It's too dangerous, Kell," Bernadette agreed. Though she looked down to Grace as she said it.

"There isn't time," Kell said.

Grandad locked eyes with Kell. His head nodded a fraction. "You save that little girl, Kell."

The look of determination on Kell's face belied the terror he felt inside. He managed a quick nod then lowered himself over the edge.

"I'll get help," Bernadette yelled. Kell saw her take off down the trail before his head slipped below the edge.

Kell looked down for a good foothold. The steep drop fell away before him and his heart skipped a beat. He took a deep breath. He saw a ledge running along the wall to his right. Maybe he could use it to reach Grace.

The last light of the day was almost gone, making it difficult to determine the edges of the rocks and ledges. Even those that were easily visible were slippery. He tried to place his foot directly on a good foothold with each step, looking down at Grace with every move. She still held onto the tree. *I have to get her out of that water.*

He scooted along the ledge a little faster. His arms were starting to tire, but there was no time to rest. No time for his mother's baby steps approach.

"Grace!" he yelled.

She didn't respond. He thought he saw her head move, but in the darkness he couldn't be sure. He continued along the ledge, the shadows now melting into one another. He peered hard, and saw a wide, crooked opening directly below him. It was as if black ink dripped down to form a vertical crack – its harsh jagged edges leading his eyes to the sloshing cold water below. One more step and he would have fallen in.

He had to get across, but how? He looked down at his sister again. Were her eyes closed? It was too dark to tell. He took another deep breath.

He could jump for it, which seemed dangerous if not impossible. If he fell into the water he would be no help to her. To anyone. There was no time to think. He couldn't wait any longer. *I promised Mom.*

He crouched down and grabbed the sharp outcrop at his feet. He slowly put all his weight on his hands and, despite the alarms going off inside his head, lowered himself blindly over the precipice, feeling his way with his feet. His pulse pounded in his neck, his arms, all through his body. He tried to slow down his breathing and let his arms extend. He slid his shoe across the rock face but found nothing. A stiff breeze blew needles of a nearby fir into his face.

His forearms began to tire from clinging to the crevice and he knew he needed to adjust his body or he would fall. Then it came to him. *Legs.* He had it in the Ology. The legs are the strongest muscles in the body. He just needed to find a way to use them. And Grace, too.

"Remember to rest on your legs, Gracie!" he yelled. He thought she would need to hear someone's voice right now.

Again he straightened his leg as far down as he could and felt his toes catch on what seemed to be a hole. He twisted his foot around and put some weight on it. It took some of the load off of his hands, which were quaking with exhaustion. He released one hand and shook it out below him. It felt good to rest. Then the world gave out beneath him.

Branches and stones scraped his skin as he slid down the rocky slope. Some loosened and plummeted alongside him. Pure instinct kept his hands against the wall, which stopped him from turning head-down, but the rough stone lashed and cut his hands mercilessly. He slid through some low shrubs, slowing him just enough for him to grab onto the final ledge a few feet from the water.

"Kell!" he heard a booming voice from above. "Kell?" His Grandad's voice cracked with panic.

"I'm okay," he shouted back. Sore and bruised but okay.

He heard scraping nearby. Grace. He had fallen to a ledge just above and to one side of her. The water, which had been at her knees, was now lapping at her armpits. Kell thought of the anemones and barnacles that could grip so tightly to slick, wet rock. They were made to hold strong against the relentless push and pull of the tides. Grace's human hands were not.

A large outcrop of rock hung over his head. He thought he must have bounced sideways to get there. His body felt that way, too.

"Gracie, are you okay?" he yelled. "Grace!"

She eased her head his direction, but couldn't seem to manage more.

"You chose a strange place to play," he said.

"Mmm," she managed a weak smile. "Cold."

"I'm here now," Kell reassured her.

He pushed himself from the rock and stood for a moment to gain his balance then shuffled toward her making sure his route was safe.

He sat up on the slab of rock above her, grabbed her under the armpits, and arched his back in effort. Using his legs he was able to drag her one little shelf higher. He tried the same motion again but couldn't find a good place to brace his feet. He kicked his shoes over and over on the slick rock.

If it had been any other person hanging half in the water he would never have come into this cove. But it wasn't any other person. It was Grace. And now, what he had to do next was even more terrifying.

I can't do this.

He lay his head back and looked up the shelves into the darkness. It was too far. He had barely survived the climb down. There was no way he could get them both to the top.

But Grandad was right. He had to save her. There was no one else. He took a deep breath and made an angry, determined face in the darkness.

"We're getting out of here, little sister," he whispered in her ear. He straightened up, pulled her further from the water, and began to study the rock.

He flinched when a rope with a large loop tied in the end unfurled with a loud slap next to them.

Kell grabbed for the rope. He felt it dance in and out of his fingers, but got a good hold and pulled the loop around his waist. He pulled Grace onto her feet and maneuvered her in front of him. Her teeth chattered and her lips looked blue, from what he could see in the darkness. Holding her upright with one arm, he looped the rope under their armpits. He pulled her tightly against him, locked one arm around her midsection, and put one arm on the rope above them.

"We're ready," he called up.

The rope grew taut. Kell leaned closer to the wall to pull on the rope and use his legs to climb. The first tug yanked them into the rock. He was able to keep Grace's face away from the hard surface but a jutting rock bashed his chin. "Mmrgh," he grunted.

"Wait!" he yelled.

The rope slackened. He repositioned his feet and again pulled Grace into a tight embrace.

Lean back away from the wall, Kell told himself. *Let the work come from above.* Leaning back toward that dark, frigid water terrified him, but he felt his shivering sister and forced himself to let his weight fall back. The rope grew taut again as it took his weight. Kell looked up. He thought of the cord as an extention of his arm, reaching all the way up the cliff. The idea helped him relax into the rope.

"Ready!" he yelled. A gentle force came from above. As they rose, Kell used his feet to guide them. It was like walking up the wall.

"I would miss you if you weren't around, Gracie," he whispered.

He could tell it was difficult for her, but she tried to move her feet.

Bernadette let out two audible gasps as Kell shifted their bodies to avoid obstacles on the cliff. Grandad's voice drifted down from above.

"Keep it up, Kell. You're doing great!" Kell sensed the compliment from the top of the cliff. He moved his feet to the last footholds and found a surge of strength in his arms to pull them up.

They reached the top. Many hands reached for them, easing them both to the ground and untangling them from the rope. Grandad took Grace's weakened body and wrapped her gently in wool blankets on a makeshift gurney another local had brought.

A few islanders Kell didn't recognize patted him on the back as the others tended to Grace. Kell was surprised to see the Jones' in the group, too.

Bernadette jumped across the circle of people. She pulled Kell to her and kissed the top of his head. Her long hair brushed against his cheek. He expected to feel the heat of a blush on his cheeks, but it did not come. The chill and pain that ran through him was deep. He melted into her.

An EMT checked Grace over and determined she had a few bumps, scrapes, and a mild case of hypothermia. He cleared her to go home after Grandad promised to give his granddaughter plenty of warm liquids, blankets, and rest for the next couple of days.

The evening's adventure was over, and the small crowd began to disperse. But the Jones brothers stayed. The twins stood looking at Kell. *Great,* Kell thought, *now they're going to get Grandad mad at me again for fighting.*

But instead of their usual vengeful or indifferent expressions, their faces seemed to have a look of admiration.

"Sorry about your sister," they said together. "We're glad she's okay."

Kell nodded in thanks. Others spoke too, but Kell didn't hear them. He was checking on Grace. "Are you okay?" he whispered. The concerned look on his face was the same as their mother's. Grace opened her eyes and offered a slight nod. She regarded her brother with thankful eyes and let them close again. Kell rubbed her forehead with his fingers, leaned down, and touched his forehead to hers. "Get some rest, Gracie."

"Let's get her home," Grandad said.

28

The next morning a breeze hummed along the shore, and a peaceful sun shone on a lone cloud. A bald eagle alighted on a tall snag, surveyed the scene for a moment, and then dove toward an unsuspecting fish. The water was calm, shimmering in the morning light.

Even during the summer the waters were more than cold enough to quickly deplete a human body of energy—even life. The tide had tossed Grace's little body in the icy water for twenty minutes. Though she had avoided the worst of it by keeping her arms and head above water—and likely kept herself alive long enough for help to arrive by doing so—the experience had taken its toll.

Grandad said what made Dead Man's Cove dangerous were the shelves. When paying attention one could easily tell the tide was coming in, but unless you read the tide tables it never let you know how high. It crept in low at times; at other times it came in higher than expected deceptively fast. Grace's first swim in the waters off Mobray was during one of the highest tides in eight years.

She was exhausted. She was draped over the couch, with only her tired face and tousled hair peeking from the pile of blankets.

Kell hadn't fared much better. He had large scrapes all along the left side of his body where he had fallen down the cliff, and his right side was badly bruised from the final impact. His arms and hands were scraped and bloody.

Grandad and Bernadette doted over the two of them as if they were injured war heroes. He and Grace were huddled near the fire smothered in blankets. Crockpot nuzzled the covers aside, not to demand his spot, but to lick their toes. All the books Kell had wanted to read during marbles games were piled nearby. Bernadette had picked them out and brought them over. As much as he ached, Kell had never enjoyed the cozy cabin more.

Later that morning, when Grandad finally left them alone to visit the outhouse, Kell limped out to tend to the chickens. But by three-o'clock, despite Grandad's fretting, Grace insisted on seeing them. "They'll help me get better, Grandad," she said. Kell had to admit she perked up when she first squeezed Moosie in her arms. She scratched under Moosie's neck and nuzzled her nose into the bird's feathers as much as Moosie would tolerate.

She gained strength as the afternoon wore on and wanted to stay outside, but Grandad shooed her to the couch. Bernadette lured her back with more bedside folktales. She demanded the Seagull and Raven tale four times in a row, but Bernadette made her promise not to use Raven's tactics on anyone again.

Late in the evening Bernadette left to deliver the weekly mail. Islanders would be waiting. They complained when their mail was not punctual. She stood on the porch and gave Kell the second smothering hug in as many days. She stood back from him and glanced toward Grace through the window. "I guess now we know why it's called Dead Man's Cove." She shook her head and sighed. She stepped down and turned around, "Oh, Kell, I almost forgot. This came for you." She pulled a letter from her back jeans pocket and handed it to him. It was from the U.S. Army Center for Military History. "I'll let you know when the other one comes in." She winked and walked off.

Kell and Grandad sat on each end of the couch. Grace's head was on a pillow in Grandad's lap and her legs lay across her brother. Crockpot was stretched out on the floor with his head on Kell's foot. One of his shoes was moist with drool and the other withstood the slow, uneven beat of the dog's tail. Crockpot's old glazed eyes followed the paths of birds that fluttered around on the front porch and outside the kitchen window. The only other sound was Kell turning the pages of his book.

Kell set the letter on the floor. He didn't have the energy to read it yet. He was already reading the same paragraph in his book over and over, seeing the words without really processing them. His mind was on the cove. The slip from the rock, branches whipping his face. It was all a frightening blur. He was shaken, too. He hadn't said much since they'd returned.

One of the chickens clucked outside.

"Never liked those birds," Grandad said. He spoke with a soft sincerity to which they weren't accustomed. His voice poured over them like warm honey.

"Your grandma named the last batch. Whenever one dies, I name the next one the same damn thing."

He looked at Grace. "Sorry." Kell wasn't sure which he was apologizing for, swearing or not liking chickens.

"It's okay," Grace said.

"You remind me a' her," he said to her.

Grace closed her eyes with a soft smile and sunk her head deeper into the pillow.

"That's why I make chicken, you know. It was our little joke. She taught me t'make it when she got sick 'a cookin'," he smiled. A tear ran down his cheek.

"God, I miss her," the old man said. His eyes glistened and he seemed to be looking past everything.

An ember popped in the stove.

"We used to dance in here," he said.

Kell wasn't sure what to say so he said nothing.

"She hated the name Dead Man's Cove. She said it was too pretty a place. Wild but pretty. Always wanted to call it Hornby Cove."

"Why Hornby Cove?" Kell asked.

"Your Grandma studied the war those final couple of years. Read everything she could. Hornby was a young naval officer, and when some of his superiors gave him orders that he thought might make things worse, he ignored a couple of them to keep the peace. She said it took guts to do what he did," Grandad looked at Kell. "Like the guts you showed yesterday."

This grumbly old man with bushy eyebrows sang in the woods and had danced around the kitchen table. That was hard enough to picture. Now he was calling Kell courageous. No one had ever called him that. His parents complimented him on an assignment or a project or how smart he was, but they had never called him brave.

The warm air of the room moved around them. After a while Grandad placed the marbles board on the old card table. Without a word, Kell and Grace set up the rickety wooden chairs from the corners of the cabin to join him. Crockpot didn't appreciate the move and groaned as he padded across the room to plunk down on colder floorboards, his chin on Gracie's feet. The tumble of the dice blended with the crackle of the fire. The heron sounded a call to its mate outside.

29

When Kell opened the letter he found Edgecumbe's name between soldiers Eager and Etherton. Edward Edgecumbe was a 2nd lieutenant originally from Glastonbury, England. The list confirmed that he had served at English Camp on San Juan Island starting in 1865, but listed no discharge date, as was given for many of the other officers. When Kell called the center to find out why, the historian said he was likely a deserter as "many of them were" during The Pig War.

Kell couldn't locate McFarlane's name anywhere, despite scouring the pages numerous times. McFarlane could have been a civilian or an American soldier. Kell would have to wait for the American Army Center's response to confirm that.

The journal seemed more legitimate now, not just a thing they had found. It was a historical document that matched up with real records from a government office. Kell had asked if the center might want to preserve it, and they were very interested. Of course, he planned on asking what Grandad wanted to do with it first.

•

The three of them—Grace, Kell, and Grandad—were sitting on the steps at Bernadette's. The past few days they had spent a lot of time together, and every morning went for a walk to town. Kell would talk to Bernadette while Grace walked to the cemetery with Grandad where they held hands, took turns wearing her cape, and did silly dances around Grandma Gert's grave. Then they would sit down under the tree and Grandad would tell her stories about his wife.

Today they had brought Grandma Gerty's box to the store to show Bernadette the rest of the items.

"Gert had always known of the journal in her childhood house while growin' up," Grandad said. "It was the old 'family diary.' It was in a baggie and lay underneath the napkins in the dining room chest of drawers for years." He turned it over. The plastic crinkled in his fingers. "It was only the past couple of years that she got interested in the man who had written it. She was readin' like a woman possessed."

"So that's what all those packages were for. Books. I always wondered," Bernadette confessed. "She never wanted to talk about it."

Grandad continued, "She knew some of her ancestors were smugglers. Gert's mama didn't think their relations would look at deserters or smugglers too kindly, so they weren't allowed to talk about it. It had been passed down that Edgecumbe started doing it to pay the bills after he deserted. He knew what kinds of things the soldiers wanted, having been one himself."

"I bet people would have been more forgiving than they thought. Especially the locals," Bernadette noted. "Islands are notorious for illegal activities. I'll bet many old-time families around here have colorful histories."

"Probably even the Jones twins," Kell offered.

"Maybe, Kell, maybe." Bernadette rubbed his hair back.

Grace took the gloves from the box and put them on. "Look, I'm a lobster," and her hands became large claws to grab all of their knees.

"Grandma loved gardening, right?" Kell said. "I remember her talking about it in Portland."

"We both did," Grandad replied.

Grace tried to pinch his knee with her gloves, but her fingers weren't big enough. "Tiny claws. You're more of a hermit crab than a lobster," he said. She squealed as he grabbed her and pulled her in for a hug.

"Why was Grandma's box hidden in the shed?" Kell asked.

"Couldn't look at it," he mumbled. "Still hard." Grace slipped off his lap and went to the box.

"I bet she wore this all the time," Grace said, holding the necklace to her chest with her claws.

Grandad turned her around, put it around her neck, and carefully fixed the clasp.

"Yep," he nodded.

"Something I still don't get," Kell said. "The pistol is probably from The Pig War, right?"

"Most likely," Bernadette said, "yes."

"So why did it end up here? If Edgecumbe moved here from the war, why doesn't it have *his* initials? What was he hiding?"

"I don't know, Kell, but I hope you find out," Bernadette answered.

"I have a question, too," Grace asked.

"Yes, Gracie," Bernadette answered.

"You said the war for pigs is important because people talked instead of fought, right?"

"Right."

"And you should talk to people even when you are angry with them, right?"

"Right."

"Well, when Kell was fighting with the Jones brothers, was that good or bad?"

Grandad smirked, and Bernadette laughed. Kell looked uncomfortable, but he felt a stab of pride, too. He had never really gotten into a fight before, and he had sort of won.

Bernadette smiled. "It's a good question, Gracie. What do you think?"

"Wait, I have another question." Grace took Grandad's hand. "Why didn't *you* ever visit us in Portland?" She scrunched up her face and shook her fist in mock anger.

He shrugged, "I hate crossin' the water."

Kell guffawed, "You live on an island, Grandad."

Bernadette tried to cover her smile with her hand.

"Didn'cher Grandma ever tell y'that?" the old man asked.

"No," Kell said.

Grace shook his arm back and forth to make his arm skin wiggle, "Did you tell her not to, Grandad? Were you embarrassed?"

"Didn't really say much about it," Grandad answered.

"That so doesn't surprise me," Kell said.

Grandad arched his eyebrows high on his forehead. "Yowzer," he said.

They all broke into laughter.

"Those are all very good questions, my new favorite family," Bernadette chuckled, "Very good questions indeed, and I think we should all discuss them over some ice cream. There is a store nearby and I just happen to know the owner."

30

It took **Kell and Grace** two hours to get to San Juan Island, on a trip to the Friday Harbor City Museum. The rickety ferry that had started their summer delivered them to the *Yakima*, a larger member of the fleet, which took them from Orcas the rest of the way to Friday Harbor. Grandad still wouldn't leave Mobray to come with them, and had only agreed to let them go alone if they met up with an old friend of his, Gene, at the ferry terminal. Gene was a retired ferryboat captain and was happy to help. Kell thought it odd that Grandad was concerned now, after giving them an entire summer of freedom, but he let it go. It was nice to have him worry a little.

•

Hidden away inside the city museum was a room off the main hallway. It was easy to miss if you didn't have reason to go there. The grand entrance drew your eyes upward and pushed you past the narrow door on the right. But if you took the time to notice and walk in, trapped beneath plexiglass were artifacts dug up mostly by construction crews over the years.

A pistol was displayed in the center of the room. A small plaque underneath stated when and where it had been found and that it had belonged to a soldier from the Pig War.

It turned out that the Jones twins had known almost as much about the weapon as the San Juan Island historian. When they finally came, in the days following the near disaster at the cove, to apologize for stealing it and generally being nasty and unneighborly—with their uncle standing right behind them—they told him what that they knew.

"It's a .44 Remington revolver," said Big Jones.

"I still think it's a Colt," said Small Jones. Big Jones punched him. Small Jones rubbed his shoulder and continued, "And it was made around 1860."

"It is amazing that you found it," Small Jones said.

"Totally amazing," Big agreed. "Not sure how we never did."

"It used gunpowder, but we aren't totally sure how it was loaded. Probably powder, wadding and a ramrod," Small offered.

"Maybe," Big said.

"But we don't know," Small replied.

"Not really," Big added.

"Gotta be from The Pig War though," they said simultaneously.

An original map of American Camp was posted on the wall nearby. Kell didn't mind that Edgecumbe's name wasn't anywhere. Finding a piece of history was its own reward, Bernadette reassured him. The local National Park historians at the museum had held a small ceremony of appreciation on San Juan Island. The *Seattle Times* and the *San Juan Islander* both had a story.

•

After leaving the museum, Kell had one more stop to make. Grace told Kell she didn't want to go see what they had come for. She was done with the "old stuff" for the summer, so she stayed behind to spend some time on the local playground with "a real live captain." Soon she had made him captain of the swingset, and herself a pirate queen challenging him to a duel.

Kell caught the local shuttle bus and headed across the island. When it stopped, he descended the steps and read the sign that stood in front of him.

English Camp

He walked up the trail toward Young Hill. As he hiked, a tunnel of Bracken ferns engulfed him, then fell away to reveal tiny shrubs sprinkled with pink flowers on stalks that rose to his waist. Young saplings reached for the sky as wise old Douglas firs towered above them. They all stood quietly to watch his solo parade.

In the last few weeks Kell had checked out books through the inter-library loan and read everything he could find on The Pig War. He talked with Bernadette about details of the occupation. His Ology was full of facts and copied pages. Now, instead of reading about the history, he wanted to see it.

"Paths were worn across the island between the two camps," he had read. "Commanders approached the other side of the island to discuss any dispute. They never thought it was the other's responsibility to approach first. They were straight with one another despite their differences, and often despite orders from their commanders."

That was what his Grandma had liked about Hornby's behavior early in the dispute. He was ordered to take action against the enemy, but chose to wait. Someone else could have been on duty on that day in the bay—someone who might have found it easier to fire first and blame the Americans later. Took guts, Grandma said.

Higher up the hill, the firs gave way to Garry oak trees and long grass that tickled his legs. Kell never knew there could be so many shades of light brown in tall waving grass.

He reached the largest oak of all and stepped to a small white picket fence enclosure. The first gravestone he approached read:

In Memory

Of

Rowan F. McFarlane

American Camp, 2nd Lieutenant

Aged 28 Years

February 16, 1866

Accidentally shot by his dear friend.

ERECTED

As a mark of esteem by fellow comrades, both English and

American.

Kell opened his backpack and found his Ology. He flipped through the dictionary and found "esteem – respect and admiration, typically for a person." No wonder McFarlane was the only American honored with a burial at the English Camp cemetery. They liked him.

All the gravestones that surrounded him—and there were only seven— were deaths that occurred during the Pig War. They were inscribed with things like "accidentally drowned" or "suddenly departed." McFarlane was one of three actually shot by the enemy, and each death was the result of a tragic mistake, not anger at all. The Pig War wasn't a war. It was a bunch of people that were supposed to fight one another, but ended up hanging out for twelve years, having discussions, and making mistakes. Kind of like a family.

His dictionary told him many useful things—that a frog was "a tailless amphibian with short stocky body and long legs for jumping" and that "an instrument for writing or drawing with ink" was a clear way to describe a pen. It defined things. Objects were easy to describe. People were complicated. Instead of an old bitter man just being "grumpy," you had to consider "dedicated," "tidy," perhaps even kind of "awesome." A little girl who was almost always "annoying" also deserved "amazing," "sweet," and "warrior." The word "war" was about "enemies" and "arms" but to that list Kell added "friends."

Kell looked east. The shimmering blue-gray water reached its liquid tendrils inland. Islands dappled the waters like immovable barges, their cargo a thick coating of live fir trees. Farther out in the sound, Canada's Gulf Islands were visible just past Haro Strait. Thanks to a German arbitrator—Grace's "Kaiser roll"—the Strait was now the dividing line between Canada and the United States. The Olympic Mountains provided a backdrop to it all.

Kell pulled out the letter from the U.S. Army Center. McFarlane's name was highlighted on the attached list between deep creases where it had been folded and unfolded. The Irishman had served the same time as Edgecumbe, though in American Camp on the other end of the island. In Kell's Ology were the notes he had used to come up with the likely scenario. With Grandad and Bernadette's help, Kell wrote it all down in a letter to send to the San Juan Island historical society. He had enclosed the original journal as a donation to the museum, as well. Grandad told him he didn't need it anymore.

Dear San Juan Historical Society and Museum,

I have included a journal that has been in my family for a long time. A man named Edward Edgecumbe wrote it. He was a soldier with the Royal Marines and likely deserted (that means left the army without permission). I have also included a pistol, which I found in a deep hole on Mobray Island, which is likely where Edgecumbe went after he deserted. Some local island experts believe the gun is a Remington. We believe Rowan McFarlane owned the pistol (note the initials on the pistol) and served at American Camp on San Juan Island from 1863-1865. His full name was Rowan Firth McFarlane. He was Irish, as many American soldiers were back then (which you probably know), and served at American Camp as a 2nd Lieutenant until 1865. We also are pretty sure that McFarlane and Edgecumbe knew one another and were even close friends.

During a hunting expedition, Edgecumbe using McFarlane's gun accidentally shot and killed his friend. The piece of paper in the plastic baggie has been in my grandmother's family for a long time and we just found it in her belongings. It was a page from Edgecumbe's journal that had fallen out long ago. The phrase when put together says, "McFarlane's dead. my frend is gone and it is my falt."

It was an accident. I'm sure Edgecumbe was very sorry. I would be, too.

Sincerely,

Kell Stepler

31

The ramp lifted to release them and the ferry eased away from the dock. The smell of saltwater was on the breeze.

"C'mon," Grace said, and she began to dodge through the few passengers. "Look Kell," she yelled back, "the back is the front again." She ran off to chat with a white-haired woman, the wind blowing their hair. He saw his sister beam when the woman bent down and commented on Grace's necklace.

They pushed into the harbor. Kell looked back over the ferry's wake at the island on which they had spent the entire summer. His mother had called yesterday. She and Dad were at the airport, about to take off for home. She said they'd fly into Houston, where they hoped to catch a direct flight to Seattle, and then rent a car to pick them up. She said she couldn't wait to see them. Dad was excited, too.

Grandad agreed to visit Portland soon. Grace took all of his marbles just to be sure. She said he would get them back once he arrived. She did say he could keep the cape at the cabin, just in case he felt like having an adventure. She left it on the hook by the door.

Kell was happy to be going home, but he was going to miss Mobray Island. He had come to love Grandad's potatoes, the tiny cabin, and the now-familiar birdcalls—even the smell of the outhouse pit. Grandad had given them a long hug at the dock. He had asked them if they wanted him to ride along to Orcas, and though Kell noticed it was more likely something the old man would be doing for himself than for them, Grace said no. Kell figured she just wanted a little more of her summer freedom. Kell felt sad for Grandad that the old man would be alone again, but most of all Kell felt sad for Edgecumbe. For a man who made a friend, then lost him, and had to live with it for a long time. Kell was proud to have a smuggler in his family, and no one could tell him otherwise.

The rear window of the ferry framed the island. Grace returned to the row of seats and snuck into a chair just as Kell was setting his pack on it. She knocked his bag to the floor, its contents spilling across the linoleum. He squished in the chair beside her and dug his elbow into her ribs. She giggled.

"It's mine," they said together, while Mobray Island slipped away.

Acknowledgements

Writing a novel is much like boarding a ferry to a mysterious island – both hold unknown adventures. Many people helped me on this journey. I'd like to thank them here.

A huge thanks goes to Elisha Cooper for early guidance and editing expertise. His support and friendship over the years have been instrumental in my coming to consider myself a writer. He also painted the beautiful cover.

To early readers for taking the time to see bigger things in an incomplete manuscript (and I mean incomplete): Cecilia Traum, Duffy Lord, Baris Cetinok, Megan Lawrence, Sara Mockett, Alice Baggett, Pete Stolpe, and Josh Spanogle. Thanks to Aaron Hoff, Mary Elder, John Roach, Brian Crawford, and Melissa Denny for helpful conversations.

Mike Vouri at the San Juan Island National Historical Park provided useful research materials as well as comments on ideas' historical accuracy. His books on the Pig War helped inspire a plot where none existed. Thanks to Jim Brown and Mary Ingraham-Brown for suggesting folk tales and Paul Mockett for one of his many ditties.

142

Special thanks to Jay Thornton for reading a draft and helping me hash out ideas many times after our respective kids were finally in bed. Debbie Pearson and Jane Slade offered invaluable editing help late process. Thanks to Jane Hesslein for serendipitous cover research. Thank you to Jason Black for his expertise and intellectual generosity and to Barney Latimer, whose professional, supportive suggestions coaxed some late changes out of me when I was spent. Thanks to David Joneschild for his name, and "Sound" knowledge. Thanks to Jud for his Judness.

Thank you to Western WA SCBWI, PNWA, Seattle7Writers, and Hugo House for supporting Pacific Northwest writers. Much appreciation to Arthur Whiteley and all involved at The Whiteley Center at Friday Harbor Labs and to the Dehlendorf's for the suggestion and the strawberries.

Exceptional thanks go to my mom, dad, sister, and all of my family for doing everything, forever, all the time. To Alice and Luke, may you have many of your own summer adventures.

Most of all, this book is for Carolyn. I thank her for everything. This book would simply not exist without her unwavering support.

The Real Pig War

Mobray Island and the characters in this book are fictional. The Pig War, however, is not. Both the American and English armies occupied San Juan Island for twelve years after an American farmer, Lyman Cutlar, shot an English-owned pig digging in his garden.

The path worn between the two camps was real.

For more information read Mike Vouri's accounts: *The Pig War*, part of Arcadia Publishing Company's Images of America series; *The Pig War: Standoff at Griffin Bay*; and *Outpost of Empire: The Royal Marines and the Joint Occupation of San Juan Island*.

Or go to the National Park Service website at http://www.nps.gov/sajh/historyculture/the-pig-war.htm

You can reach the author at www.markholtzen.com.

17026272R00078

Made in the USA
Charleston, SC
23 January 2013